"I am pretty sure we can get this part at the hardware store."

Taking a break from everything that reminded him of his unknown future would be good for him. "Promise I know the way." Jack nudged her with his elbow.

Molly gave him a surprised look. "You don't remember, do you? You said those exact words on our way to Alfonso's for homecoming, and we got stuck clear on the other side of town."

Oh man, Jack had totally forgotten that, but now he remembered that *promise I know the way* became an inside joke every time she got in his truck after homecoming.

"That was a great night, Mol." He watched her face soften. Why'd he feel like somehow he'd jumped all the way back to the quarterback standing in the middle of his girlfriend's living room?

At least he knew that Molly was no longer the girl who dated the quarterback. She was all grown up and establishing her career and her own dream. He was thankful she'd found her way…without him.

Angie Dicken credits her love of story to reading British literature during life as a military kid in Cambridgeshire, England. Now living in the American heartland, she blogs about author life along with her fellow Alley Cats on *The Writer's Alley* blog. Besides writing, she is a busy mom of four and works in adult ministry. Angie enjoys eclectic new restaurants, authentic conversation with friends and date nights with her Texas-native husband. Connect with her online at www.angiedicken.com.

Books by Angie Dicken

Love Inspired

Once Upon a Farmhouse

Love Inspired Historical

The Outlaw's Second Chance

Visit the Author Profile page at LoveInspired.com.

Once Upon a Farmhouse

Angie Dicken

LOVE INSPIRED
INSPIRATIONAL ROMANCE

LOVE INSPIRED®
INSPIRATIONAL ROMANCE

Recycling programs
for this product may
not exist in your area.

ISBN-13: 978-1-335-58523-3

Once Upon a Farmhouse

Copyright © 2022 by Angie Dicken

For questions and comments about the quality of this book, please contact us
at CustomerService@Harlequin.com.

Love Inspired
22 Adelaide St. West, 41st Floor
Toronto, Ontario M5H 4E3, Canada
www.LoveInspired.com

Printed in U.S.A.

I will turn their mourning into joy,
and will comfort them, and make them
rejoice from their sorrow.
—*Jeremiah* 31:13

In loving memory of Gran and Big Dad,
two very special farmhouse owners.

And in honor of our favorite superhero, Brady.
Keep up the fight against CF!

Chapter One

Molly Jansen inched her face toward the steering wheel and tilted her head in the direction of the radio. She nodded along with the podcast about sustainable architecture, convincing herself that the little leap in her stomach was evoked by the speaker's mention of solar panels, not by the big block letters of *The People of Iowa Welcome You* screaming from the sign on the steel bridge.

No matter how much she accomplished, *those* people were her people. Regardless of her effort, crossing the Mississippi River in her sporty Civic drowned out all she had become—a Notre Dame honors graduate, an independent Chicago urbanite and an ambitious junior architect. Yet, no potential promotion in her career would redefine the small-town Iowa girl of her past.

Molly wasn't sure she was completely okay with that—or with some of those people here in Iowa. Weren't they part of the reason she left, anyway?

Her playlist of various podcasts mingled with thoughts of those last moments with Granddad in that hospital room a couple weeks ago. More than once during this five-hour car trip, she questioned her decision to rush her visit after his accident. Nobody was aware that he would never leave that room. Molly would have stayed longer if she had known. Exactly why she left Chicago this time without a return date. It was the least she could do for Gran. Molly settled back and focused on old eighties hits streaming from her phone. But when she pulled down the gravel drive and faced the two-story farmhouse with dingy white siding and missing roof shingles, her nerves just couldn't be ignored. She shuddered at the reality that Granddad would not come out to greet her. And as she parked in her usual spot after a decade of being away, she began to shrink inward.

"Stop it, Molly. You are here to help Gran. Nobody needs a visit. No trips down memory lane." Her pep talk was a hollow echo. She may as well have been sitting in her 2001 Mercury Sable cluttered with empty fountain drink cups and football-ticket stubs. The same ol' gravel dust settled on the car hood, the same tall green rows of corn lined the edge of the drive, and the sky was just as blue and broad as every Iowan claimed as perfection.

Molly tumbled out of her bucket seat and grabbed her hard-shell roller from the back. She set it down with a crunch on the white pebbles of her childhood play yard. No doubt, her wedges stood on the exact spot where she'd sloshed through the soupy puddles in her rubber boots, dragging a wagon filled with drenched sweet corn during that summer the whole county seemed to flood. Of course, now, as a grown woman, she realized her chore had been assigned to keep her distracted while her grandad and father discussed the severe damage done.

She wasn't here to survey crops or keep busy while the real farmers talked.

"What I would give for that." Molly ran her hand

through her straightened shoulder-length hair, thinking on the similar near-black color of her grandfather's curls poking out from beneath his John Deere cap. Before they peppered and went gray in her teen years. "Miss you, Grandad." She squinted past the house at the towering corn plants, wrangling the tears that pushed behind her eyes and the groan that curdled in the back of her throat.

"Ten years?" A rich baritone voice traveled from somewhere in the rows. She noticed a hat, not unlike her grandad's. Molly was too practical to believe that her imagination was running wild, but her skin tingled at a familiarity she just couldn't shake—

Then, she saw *him.*

"Jack?" Her lip hooked on both sides as if she'd just caught a whiff of the hog barn down the road. Immediately, she smacked her mouth shut and goggled at the tall, suntanned Jack Behrens emerging from the corn like some *Field of Dreams* baseball player. But instead of a pinstriped uniform, he wore a taut—much too taut— Iowa State University T-shirt with the sleeves cut off, as if those biceps just couldn't stand being constricted anymore. Molly glanced down at her roller bag, gripped the handle with all her might and cleared her throat. "What are you doing here?"

Jack strode toward her, hooking his thumbs in his jean pockets. "I kinda expected to see you a little sooner."

If her memory was still sharp, beyond her effort to dull it, a cocky half smile would set off a sparkle in those brown eyes as he volleyed the subject to her. But Jack hardly smiled. She saw no sparkle from beneath the dark shade of the faded green bill.

"I visited Grandad at the hospital after the accident. I had no idea it was so serious..." She diverted her gaze to the ground between them. Shaking her head, she tried to focus on the rocks and dirt. "If I had known…" She grimaced and stepped back, tossing her hair behind her shoulders. "When did you see him last?" She slowly looked up at him, the brim of his hat pulled even lower than before.

His chin pushed up his bottom lip into a firm pout, and he sniffed. "Same day. The accident wasn't that bad, but they didn't expect infection."

Molly could only nod. Gran had told her that much. Farming accidents were not as common as they used to be, but the possibility was never far from a farmer's mind. With such a wise and careful man like her grandad, she never thought it could happen to him. Especially after retirement. Although, the man lived and breathed farming. Retirement hadn't slowed him down much. Every time Molly called between Memorial Day and harvest, Grandad was out in the fields, tinkering around.

The grinding roar of a crop duster relinquished the awkward silence between her and Jack. They both looked up and watched the small yellow plane sail across the sky toward the McMillan farm down the way.

Molly sighed and tightened her grip on the smooth black handle. "I'll stay a while after the funeral. Gran and Grandad agreed they would sell the place once he recovered…but since…" Molly fluttered her lashes, shaking her head. "I am going to help Gran get it ready to sell." A funeral and a home makeover were the reasons she was here. Not to take a trip back to hot summer days on the farm or cool fall nights waiting for Jack after the football game. She'd have to say both memories had been tucked away for a good long while, but the latter was one she had hoped to forget. She yanked her bag and started rolling it toward the house.

Jack jogged up and walked beside her. "You know, there really is no need to sell right now. I am here to help her with whatever she needs."

Molly pushed her chin into her neck and gawked at him. "What exactly are you doing here, Jack? This is Austin property. I believe you're a little far from home." Molly was the one who smirked. Yeah, it felt good to enlist her grown-up confidence in the face of this man. Jack could make her melt like a giddy woman in one of those black-and-white films that Gran made her suffer through while they waited up for Grandad during harvest. Not anymore. "Thought you'd be up to your elbows managing the Corn Crib by now."

He chuckled. Still no sparkle, though. He lifted the hat with one hand and raked his hand back through his honey-brown hair with the other. "Nope. Got a degree in agribusiness, not restaurant management." His Adam's apple bobbed against his fraying collar. "Besides, Dad's retired. Sold the restaurant, and it became a pizza chain." He shook his head. "Smack dab in the middle of an Iowa small-town square."

"Wow. That's too bad. Best tenderloin in the county." There wasn't much to the nearby town of Polk Center. But the square was idyllic with its general store, flower boutique, a smattering of offices and the pride and joy of farming diners, the Corn Crib. "And you are here, doing business…in agriculture?" Instead of a smirk, she went ahead and flashed a full-on smile.

He stepped in her path with one quick shuffle, standing between her bag and the steps to the front porch. "Let me take that." He swiped off his hat, releasing a faint waft of whatever shampoo or hair product he used. Cedar and a hint of mint. Molly managed not to inhale too deeply, against her very wavering will. Jack tucked his hat in his back pocket and reached for the roller bag.

"Uh, no thanks." Quickly, she sidestepped him and hurried to the first step.

"Oh yeah, heard you'd become a city girl."

"If being a city girl means being able to handle a little bag up a couple of steps—" Molly lugged it up as effortlessly as she could feign "—then, you are very right." Only a few more seconds of this time warp and she'd be inside Gran's kitchen, ready to figure out the Wi-Fi hook up.

"Architect, right?"

"Yes, I am." Molly glanced at her phone. "And I need to get inside. Gran's texting to see where I am." She raised her eyebrows, unable to ignore the fact that her ex-boyfriend stood in the exact same spot when they'd last said goodbye. He was nearly the same as she remembered. A little thicker in the waist but no less muscular. His arms had busted out of those sleeves, hadn't they? Yet, there was something incredibly soft about him. His brow seemed to break upward more than it ever had. Even when he smiled.

"Well, Molly Jansen, I'll be seeing you." He crammed his hat on, pulling it down low over his eyes, then pushing it up. Like peekaboo with those almost amber gems. "It's about time to get back to the crew."

"Crew?"

"Yep. Wade Grover's detasseling the back half."

"Back half of what?"

Now his eyes did sparkle. Molly followed his gaze across the side yard of Gran's detached garage to the southern quarter section of corn. She could barely see the top of a truck in the dirt road that lined the back. "You have a detasseling business?"

"Nah." He shoved his hands in his pocket. "I farm this land."

"What?" Molly whipped around to face him. "I thought Gran said they had hired a—"

"A farm manager?" Now his sparkle was a full-on shine. His lopsided smile appeared, and he rocked back on his heels. "Agribusiness, remember?"

"So you took over when Grandad retired," Molly mumbled. "What are you going to do now that we're selling it?" Her throat tightened as she realized all this time away, he had been closer to her family than she had.

"Try to convince you not to?" His smile faded. A ripple of desperation extinguished the sparkle in his eyes. "Mol, I'd buy it if I could." He said it as if all his future depended on her next words. "Think you can convince Gertie?"

"I'm just here to fix the place up." She shrugged her shoulders, wondering how this man, once the boy of her dreams, could still have the same effect on her, years later. Shaky stomach, butterflies…but grown-up empathy at his heartfelt, unreasonable plea. "I have no farming sense…and this really isn't in my control." Molly glanced back at the field, then straightened her bag and looked at her watch. "See you around?"

He pressed his lips in a thin smile and dipped his chin. "See you."

Molly dragged the bag and opened the screen door slowly, waiting until Jack appeared in her peripheral and disappeared through the side door of the garage. Only once he was completely out of sight could she release all the air that was trapped in her lungs by this unexpected and, frankly, unwanted high-school reunion.

Rummaging through the toolbox, Jack just couldn't keep his thoughts untangled. Seeing Molly show up in this borrowed territory was both a surprise and a sobering reminder of all he'd lost and what he was about to lose. His eyes blurred as the tools clinked together. He avoided the sharp edge of a putty knife. Where was that wrench?

Jack rubbed the back of his neck and sucked air through his teeth, not wanting to go into the house. But he remembered the last time he'd used the wrench was to help Gertie fix her kitchen sink. He shoved the tool bag aside and stomped out of the garage into the bright summer sun.

Decades of baked bread were memorialized in the warm scent pouring from Gertie's kitchen screen door. The scent was named *home away from home* as far as Jack was concerned. He tapped his knuckles on the doorjamb, regretful to interrupt the rising chatter between a grandmother and her granddaughter. But he knew where that wrench was, and if they weren't sitting at the kitchen table, he'd just pop in and grab the tool without disturbing the two women.

"Come on in, Jack!" Gertie's voice was high-pitched. When he stepped inside, he noticed her eyes were red as she swiped at her nose with an old-fashioned handkerchief. Molly was gripping her hand across the table. Her blue eyes were teary beneath eyebrows tilted in compassion, and her lips were set in a strong smile of surrender.

"Sorry to bother you two." He jaunted over to the sink, opened the cabinet and grabbed the wrench. "I know it's a tough time." He tipped his John Deere hat as he headed to the door.

"Son, it's a tough time for you too." Gertie sniffled. She patted the table. "Come, sit with us. I have coffee brewing."

Jack exchanged glances with Molly as he approached. Her smile faded. "I have to talk through a few things with the crew manager before I pick up Tate. Besides, you all have a lot of catching up to do." He gently squeezed Gertie's shoulder. "I'll let you get to it."

Gertie placed her hand on his. "I don't know what I would do without Jack, Molly. He's been so helpful around here." She looked up at him with a quivering smile. "It's been nice to get to know this brave heart and his little boy." She winked.

Molly shifted in her seat. "Little boy? Wow, family man?"

Jack clenched his jaw and gave a curt nod. She didn't know. How could she? Why would the Austins mention him to Molly, anyway? Not after how they'd left things. If he remembered correctly, he chose to break it off when Molly's struggles with her mom clashed with his social life their senior year. Yeah, there had been no reason to mention Jack.

"So much has changed around here." Molly retrieved her hand from holding Gertie's, leaned back in her chair and looked up at him without turning her head. "I didn't even expect to see you on the property."

"Oh, we take care of each other, don't we, Jack?" Gertie turned and gave him a smile that betrayed the sadness in her eyes.

"We sure do." He filled his lungs with air, trying to avoid the many warm memories that had braided together his own sorrow with the joy of Gertie's hospitality and Rob's steady composure. They'd been there for him when he was at his weakest. "I don't know where I'd be without you and Rob. Miss him already."

The women lowered their attention to the table, and Jack shifted his weight. Even the coffeepot quieted in this moment of silence. If Rob hadn't given him a chance to work during the summers while he was at Iowa State, Jack didn't know where he'd be now. The security of a mentor who believed in him was his only pillar when life crumbled around him. Rob had offered Jack so much more than a job. He'd offered him friendship. Even though Rob was gone, Gertie was going to continue with their plan to move closer to the city to her sister's retirement community.

Finally, Gertie sighed loudly and said, "Coffee's done."

Jack rubbed his cheek, trying to figure out how to excuse himself. Molly scooted her chair back and passed behind him quickly. She opened the fridge door and pulled out the creamer.

"Gran, we might have to buy some new appliances for showings. You can take the fridge with you but—"

"I am here for you, Gertie," Jack blurted. "No need to rush things around here." He glanced about the kitchen with the dull oak trim and the water-stained ceiling. Another goodbye looming ahead threatened to rip to shreds his thin veil of peace. "This place is a gem. Give yourself some time."

Molly cleared her throat and tapped her fingers on the laminate countertop. "Jack, your crew is probably snoozing on the bus by now. I know I would have taken the chance if the boss disappeared back when I detasseled. Such a chore to remove those sprouts on the top of corn plants for…what was it…pollination control? I just wanted to sleep." She laughed a little forcefully, as if she was trying to lighten the mood. "Getting up at five in the morning is the worst during a high-school summer." She tucked her black hair behind her ear and winked at Gertie.

"I remember you grumbling." Gertie chuckled. It was good to hear her laugh.

"Good thing I'm not their boss. Wade's taking care of them, I'm sure." Jack slipped his hand from beneath Gertie's and eyed the back door. "But I better get going. Got lots to do before getting Tate." And he couldn't forget getting to the pharmacy before it closed. He didn't have enough meds for Tate's breathing treatment this evening. He chided himself for not being on top of these things. His wife had taken so much better care of their son's medical needs. Jack's lacking was only a reminder of her absence.

"You're still picking us up, right?" Gertie called out, her voice cracking.

"I'll be here bright and early tomorrow." Jack tipped his hat. He made a mental note to hit the car wash too. Tate would love to ride along for that—play rocket ship while the brushes washed off the grime of dirt roads.

"We'll see you then." Gertie pushed herself up from the table. "Not going to be my favorite day." She crossed over to the cabinet and grabbed some mugs. "But I am sure glad to have my two favorite people taking care of me right now." She kissed Molly on the cheek and then swiveled toward Jack. "Now, you go set those sleepy teenagers straight. We need to be sure this crop is a good one, don't we, son?" Her firm tone was reminiscent of her husband's. If there was anything Jack could do to buy up the land and keep Austin Farm a legacy, he would. But if he was completely practical, the only thing in his control was caring for this final crop. And Jack Behrens would do his best to make Rob proud—and Gertie too.

Now, Molly, on the other hand, had no idea what her family meant to him. And he hadn't thought about high school in a long time. Seemed like a lifetime ago when he and Molly had dated their senior year. Too much life had been lived, and too much had been taken away. He looked over his shoulder before slipping down the path behind the garage. He could see the back of Molly's head through the kitchen window. She was a city girl through and through—that fancy straight-as-a-board hair, the sleeveless silk blouse and her coolness that didn't fit in that well-worn home.

They had their past in common and their love for a man they'd bury tomorrow. But besides that, Molly Jansen and Jack Behrens were certainly two tractors passing through the heartland, one wearing the brakes thin, and the other stomping on the gas.

Chapter Two

"Seems like Jack is more than an employee to you."
Molly sipped her coffee. "You treat him like—"

"Family?"

Molly shrugged her shoulders. "I guess so." Could
she really judge what that meant? Life in Chicago was
all work, not a blood relative within five hours. And Dad
was down in Florida: visiting him was the best excuse to
get away from Midwest winters in December. "I didn't
expect to see my ex, that's for sure."

"I'll admit, I was surprised when he showed up nine
years ago to intern for Grandad his first summer of college. He'd not made a great name for himself in these
old walls." She glanced around at the papered walls but
landed sympathetic green eyes in Molly's direction.
"You two were like oil and water toward the end."

Molly tensed. She gripped the cup and tried to swal-
low back any residue of a broken heart. "If you recall,
Gran, that last year for me was not stellar."

She pushed her chin up and whispered, "I do." Clearing her throat, she spoke loudly, "Truth be told, this
old house seems like a hospital for broken hearts. Jack

spent many a night at this table, nursing wounds of his own, while I rocked his little boy to sleep just like I once rocked you."

"I can't believe you never told me." Molly set her cup down, and Gran opened her mouth to speak but then shrugged her shoulders. Molly offered a reassuring smile not wanting to upset her. "And Jack has a kid?" Molly shook her head. She hadn't imagined that Jack had changed. Of course, he had. He was a daddy. "What in the world's gone on around here? The high-school hotshot has a son and practically moves into his ex-girlfriend's house…the girl he dumped right before prom, by the way?" She forced a laugh to assure herself, and Gran, that she wasn't so serious about all that happened. The edge in her voice betrayed her, but still, she was definitely not the same person back then. "Seems like I've entered some sort of *Twilight Zone.*"

Gran hooked her eyebrow. "That's what happens when you stay gone. Life keeps on living 'round here for the rest of us." Her smirk grew the dimple in her ivory cheek, and she brushed her fingers along her silver hair. If one thing hadn't changed over the years, it was Gran's hairstyle. Long bangs and straight shoulder-length hair that curled under at the ends.

Her teasing smile faded, and she lowered her eyes to her own mug.

"It's not like we don't talk on the phone." Molly dismissed her grandmother's sudden solemnity and the niggle of guilt in her gut. "You've never mentioned this second grandchild-man of yours." She grinned wide.

Gran's bubbling laugh smoothed over the last of Molly's uneasiness about the topics they'd covered in such a brief welcome chat. "I talk on the phone to hear about *you*, dear. I am so proud of you." Her eyes glistened. "Grandad was so proud of you too. Would tell his friends to check out the buildings you've mentioned when they said they were traveling to Chicago."

Molly ran her finger along the rim of her mug, shaking her head slowly. "That's super sweet, but I just fix the redlines. The designers get the credit for the buildings, really." Her stomach leaped. "That actually might happen for me sooner than later." She sipped her coffee and sat back. "I hope you have good internet here. The biggest project of my life is sitting on my laptop, and I plan on it snagging me a promotion."

"Well, that is wonderful!" Gran leaned forward, then scrunched her nose. "But I am not too sure about the internet, dear. We'll see what we can do. Jack is quite the handyman."

"Okay," Molly murmured. She scooted back and took her mug to the sink. Bright sunshine bathed the crop out back, growing long shadows between the garage and the house. A ginger cat ran along the edge of the driveway and dashed under the old corn crib, disappearing into the weeds. "I can't believe the Corn Crib in town is a chain restaurant now."

"It surprised all of us. Especially Jack." Gran joined her at the sink. "His dad left right in the middle of Brittany's cancer."

"Brittany?"

"Jack's wife, dear."

Molly stepped back. "Oh, of course. The kid…a wife. Wow, Jack has grown up."

Gran nodded slowly, turned the water on and began to wash the mugs. "Shortly after Jack and Brittany moved into the old split-level house down the road, during a postpartum checkup they found out she was sick. Only been married for a couple years. Was a tough journey."

Molly turned away from the window and leaned back on the counter. "That is so difficult. How is she now?"

Gran stopped washing. She stared out the window in the direction where Jack was probably bossing around fifteen-year-olds. "The Lord's enjoying her spunkiness now. Jack is a widower, darling. The youngest I've known."

"So much *has* happened since I left." Molly's throat was tight as she glanced around the small kitchen where she once ate cinnamon rolls and watched Saturday cartoons on a black-and-white television. "No wonder Jack doesn't want you to leave."

"I know, dear." She dabbed her eyes with the back of her wrist, then continued washing. "When Grandad suggested we move away after this last accident, I was surprised. He was scared that he couldn't manage the place like he once thought. Now he's gone. And I believe his suggestion is still the best. There's been a lot of leaving this place through the years. It's about time I tried my turn at leaving it too." She chuckled. But Molly couldn't join her, having been the latest Jansen girl to leave the farm. She pushed away the guilt that had been tugging at her since she'd first stepped out of her car. She'd done nothing wrong by going off and living life. That's what kids did when they graduated high school. She was here now. And that was worth celebrating in her mind. There had been no hesitation to head to see Grandad in the hospital in Des Moines. But it had taken a lot to return to Polk Center.

After they finished up in the kitchen, Molly carried

her bag upstairs to her old room, then hurried down again to set up her laptop on the old rolltop desk in Gran's living room. She felt as though she had walked into a dollhouse. Every piece of furniture was smaller than she remembered, and the ceiling seemed lower.

"If only your father could have come for tomorrow." Gran sighed as she ambled across the hardwood floors carrying a large garment bag. She laid it out on the back of the couch and began to unzip it.

"He said to send you his love. He's sad to miss it, but he committed to caring for his ill neighbor this weekend." Molly helped her retrieve a black suit.

"He's such a good man. Okay, I'd better get this ironed. It's been shoved in my closet for a year now."

Molly slowly zipped up the empty bag while Gran fetched an ironing board and iron. Molly dreaded bringing up the question that had been rolling around in her mind since the first frantic phone call from Gran. She'd avoided thinking on it herself. Just hoping that the answer would be clear without having to voice it. And if she was honest with herself, the answer had been pretty clear. Eleven years of crystal clear. But she didn't want to run the risk of any other surprises at Grandad's funeral tomorrow. She already had to prepare to face a whole town.

Molly helped Gran lock the ironing board in place, then she plugged in the iron. "So anyone coming from out of state?" Molly pressed her lips together, as if she was waiting for her annual flu shot to sting her arm.

"Not that I know of. I mean, all of our cousins are here and—" Gran's mouth fell, and she cocked her head in a familiar gesture of sympathy. "Oh darling. I haven't heard from her either." Molly tried to remain unaffected, but her eyes stung. She rushed over to her computer, her back to the rest of the house and her grandmother. "Believe me, I pray every day for her to show up on my doorstep, begging for some kind of prodigal's return. The damage she caused to her father's heart...to mine—" Gran's voice caught on a sob.

Molly spun around and rushed over as Gran lowered to the adjacent armchair. "I am sorry to bring Mom up. I'm always wondering if that's just going to be an open wound for the rest of my life. Need to know if there's any chance of stitching it up." She huffed and sat on the arm of the chair, threading her fingers with Gran's.

"I guess I have made my peace with it, but I don't blame you for wondering one bit. She did you the most wrong."

"It was a long time ago."

"She was your mother."

"Still is, I guess."

"I think that the loss is hers." Gran squeezed her hand harder than Molly expected from her dainty fingers. "You are a fine young lady." She kissed Molly's cheek and stood. "I'd better get to ironing my suit for tomorrow. Don't think I'll have the gumption to do it in the morning."

"Sure. And I have a conference call." Molly inhaled a shaky breath, pulled out her cell from her back pocket and headed toward the chair at the desk. "I'll wrap up some stuff so tomorrow is uninterrupted." She swiveled in her seat. Gran was already consumed with the task of ironing her long black pants.

Molly turned around again, smiled at her screen saver, Frank Lloyd Wright's Fallingwater, then scrolled through her contacts. She was happy to settle back into her architecture shoes. They were a perfect fit and a chance to walk away from the places her heart sometimes dared to tread.

Jack turned from Austin Farm, eyeing the corn from his rearview mirror. There was nothing better than a long, hot day on the farm, even if the corn really did all the work. This year's crop was a beaut. He could just sit back and watch it grow all day long. And even though farmers didn't typically spend time with the seed company's detasseling crew, Jack made it a point to unofficially partner with his buddy, Wade Grover, the crew manager from the seed company.

At first, those teens had shown up with bed head and sleepy eyelids this morning, but by quitting time, they had earned their first paycheck with solid, hard work. As they left, energy was high with all the talk about the upcoming prestate baseball game. Wade teased them about the good ol' days, when there was no competition as tough as the state champs, the Polk Center Raiders of '99. The few ballplayers in the crew rattled off stats and made big promises about heading to the tourney this year.

There was definitely no sleeping on the bus like Molly had mentioned.

Jack chuckled, shaking his head as he turned onto the main road. She was nothing like he remembered. And even though he hadn't thought about their short but intense dating bout in a long time, her confidence just blew in here like a tornado, knocking down all the walls he'd put up to manage where his thinking time was spent.

Had he thought of anything past yields and forecasts and Tate's cystic fibrosis over this past year?

All afternoon, Jack's thoughts spun to the farmhouse, tempting him to recall what life had been like with Molly Jansen around Polk Center. How could someone change so unrecognizably? Big cities seemed to do that to folk.

Jack managed to pull up to the pharmacy right when they were locking up. Thankfully, the clerk helped him anyway. While the meds he picked up were at least covered by insurance, the bills waiting for him in his mailbox were not. Each bill had him tense up even more. He tossed them to the passenger-side floorboard. Would he ever get his head above this debt? All those trial treatments and chances of progress were mocking him with each past-due notice of what it had cost to hope.

He shifted his truck into Park, hopped out and ran inside. The house was quiet. Checking his phone, he groaned at a missed text from his sister, Lisa. She had taken Tate to the ball field. Her husband was the varsity coach, after all. Jack sighed. He should have gotten home on time during baseball playoffs. Lisa was nearly as avid about the team as her husband and Jack were. Everybody loved cheering on their River Raiders. He texted her quickly, made two PB&Js and headed to the baseball field.

His usual spot along the outfield fence, right of center, was free. A few familiar cars were already parked. Families were setting up bag chairs close to the fence. He waved as he got out and ran over to the Honda minivan, the tailgate yawning open smack dab at center field.

"Daddy!" Tate was sitting in his child-size folding chair, dressed in the superhero pajamas he'd worn since he was two. Two years of grocery-store trips, playground romps and snuggling on the couch at the end of a long day, and those PJs were still holding up. Although, last

Jack had checked, the pants were creeping up above his ankles. Tonight, though, Tate wore his cowboy boots, hiding one fashion statement for another.

"Hey, Tater." Jack kissed the top of his head and handed him his sandwich. "Ready to catch a homer?"

"Yes, sir." Tate held up his glove. "I've got this, Dad. See, Aunt Lisa parked in the best spot."

His sister popped her head out from the side of the van. "He insisted."

Jack walked over. She was twisting a sippy cup for eighteen-month-old Elise, who was climbing down into the tall grass. "Sorry I'm late."

Lisa shrugged. "We'd both be here no matter what. Doesn't make much difference to me to bring Tate along. You grabbed his prescription, though?" A hint of concern flashed in her near-identical-to-Jack's brown eyes.

"Got it."

"Good. He's been wheezing more than usual." She gave Elise her cup, and they all walked over to the folding chairs set up near Tate. "I think you might need to leave early and give him his treatment."

"Whatever it takes." Jack squatted beside Tate. "Good sandwich?" His little boy smiled with peanut-buttery teeth and healthy pink lips. Good, no blue. "Feeling okay?"

Tate nodded with enthusiasm. Jack couldn't help but chuckle, although his stomach twisted knowing how the energy of a four-year-old sometimes distracted from the warning signs to call the doctor or, worse, head to urgent care. After staying close, watching and listening, Jack finally sat in his own chair and finished his sandwich while warm-ups wrapped up.

"Ed's been thinking about barbecuing for some of the

old gang. You up for it tomorrow?" Lisa offered Tate a napkin, then scooped Elise up and away from an old can stuck in the chain-link fence.

Jack pressed his shoulders back and sucked air through his teeth. "I don't know. Rob's funeral is in the morning. Not sure I'll be up for socializing."

Lisa nodded. "He meant a lot to all of us, especially you. I get it." She pushed her chin up and gave a sympathetic smile.

Did she truly get it, though?

Jack wasn't just facing honoring the life of a friend. He was going to walk through familiar steps again. Entering that funeral home just the same as he'd done a year ago; finding the composure to make it through hymns and a eulogy; suffering through the condolences of folks who would just mark off their calendar at the end of the day, continue on as normal, even if it was with one less person in their life.

But Jack had to wrestle with the fact that his life would never be the same. He felt like he had finally found the ability to stand from his year-long crawl after Brittany's funeral. Now he feared Rob's death erased any kind of trajectory of a steady walk forward. What exactly was Jack walking toward?

He glanced over at Tate and admired the perfectly rounded nose sprinkled with freckles. His long lashes were just like his mama's. Tate would have to go along with Jack, whatever that forward motion might be. For Tate, though, security was a must. Even though he appeared to be a healthy little boy, to a trained eye that small hitch of his chest with each labored breath, no matter how slight, was enough to keep anxiety close at heart. Even a pretty broken heart. All the pieces overflowed with love for this little guy. And Jack's worry only grew knowing how bleak his future appeared without Rob Austin around.

Once the first inning started, Tate crawled up into Jack's lap, and they cheered for the River Raiders together. The lights slowly turned on as the sky grew pink above the outlying crops. Nothing like a Midwest evening at the ball field. Iowa was the only state with high-school baseball in the summer. A blessing, for sure.

During the sixth inning, Tate begged to go to the concession stand, so they headed over for some popcorn and lemonade. On their way back, a bunch of girls hollered for the number of the away team's pitcher in the bullpen.

"He's number ten!" Tate yelled to them.

The girls all turned red at once, then tumbled into a fit of giggles.

"Dad, it's on his shirt." Tate's eyes were as big as robin's eggs, nearly the same color, and his shoulders were up to his ears.

Jack chuckled. "Different kind of number, bud."

The pitcher was doing his best to focus on the next throw. But the hint of a smile on his face was more than familiar to Jack. He'd enjoyed the same kind of attention from the football-field sidelines. Those were the days. Some of the best.

He wasn't so sure about those days with Molly, though. If he remembered correctly, she hadn't gone to his football games much. She had missed out on the best plays he'd ever made. Even if it was for a good reason, obvious to Jack on this side of grief, he was a little uneasy thinking that he wasn't so understanding back then.

He tossed some popcorn in his mouth and forced his attention down on the brown curls above a Superman cape. Remorse surprised him as the image of Molly standing on the porch with tears streaming down her face appeared in his mind. What had he said to hurt her? He grimaced. All he could remember was their last encounter had not been a pleasant one. Their relationship was like a weed after rain. Quick to grow and stubborn to get rid of. She seemed to want to settle down, and he was having the time of his life—without her, most days.

Did it matter now? Surely after ten years it was too late to rehash it all. Everything worked out as it should. He wouldn't want to go back, anyway. Miss the chance of meeting Brittany, having Tate or finding the Austins for the second time 'round? Nah, those pieces of his life were priceless.

Besides, the new Molly certainly didn't seem interested in striking up a conversation. Jack couldn't worry about the past. If anything, Molly was here to work against his future. No, the only thing he should focus on with regard to Molly Jansen was the fact that tomorrow was going to be a tough day for both of them.

Then the hardship would be all on him the day after.

Jack would just enjoy the rest of the game with his son. At least the River Raiders were up by several runs with a fantastic sunset coloring the win. Those boys would have a lot to talk about with Wade tomorrow. Too bad Jack couldn't join them.

Chapter Three

Familiar shadows crept along the bedroom floorboards, flinging Molly back into her school days as she lay in her old twin bed beneath a subtle swath of moonlight. A cool nighttime breeze poured from her open window. She closed her eyes and inhaled the Iowa air. Dew-soaked grass and rich dark soil. A hint of rain. A trace of burning wood from some distant bonfire. There wasn't much near Gran's house. Their closest neighbor was the split-level house about two miles down the road. Now Jack lived there. Was he roasting marshmallows with his little boy?

This was all so strange.

He was one of the people she dreaded seeing most upon her return. Mom had left for good during her senior year, and instead of Molly being able to count on her boyfriend for comfort, Jack had broken up with her when she needed him most.

There was a whole bunch of others who made her miserable in high school. She searched her brain for a Brittany, praying she'd held no hard feelings toward the woman who'd passed away. Scooting up in her bed, she clicked on the lamp and pulled her yearbook from the nightstand.

Her hand trembled as she looked through the pages. Only one hundred names to scan through made her search for a Brittany easy. There wasn't one. Yet, little relief came to her with that confirmation. A whole slew of memories was gnawing at her brain, trying to emerge and knock her off the pedestal of success she'd built all on her own.

"Lord, please let none of these people be there tomorrow." She didn't want any questions, any strange looks. Her stomach churned just thinking about saying goodbye to her grandfather tomorrow. She definitely couldn't bear the commotion of old scrutiny colliding with her new grief. The last time she was going through a hard time, she was made the center of ridicule by the meanest kids out there. If only those bullies had known the dark thoughts they had provoked in her mind.

She chided herself for fearing bullies. She was an adult now. Back then, all that sorrow and anger had consumed her. Now, it bumped against full-grown confidence, yet threatened to eat it away.

Molly slammed the book shut. She was fine. Even if they asked about her, she had plenty of good things to share.

There was no use sleeping right now. She did not want to run the risk of backtracking any further, and she had a hunch that closing her eyes would do just that. She swung her legs over her bed and found her fuzzy slippers, must-haves in a drafty farmhouse.

The door creaked open. She recalled every quiet spot down the staircase, as if it was only yesterday when she would sneak out to swing on the porch with Jack, well past her grandparents' bedtime. Her shoulders slumped at one of the sweeter memories creeping up to meet her halfway down the stairs. She could barely see the chains of the swing through the window by the front door. And as she reached the last step, she gasped. A glistening pair of eyes stared through the window, nestled in the swing cushions.

"Silly cat," she whispered on a breathy giggle. As she turned toward the living room, the ball cap wobbled and fell off the newel into her hand. "Oh man, this house is literally falling apart." Molly set it on the bench by the front door, then made her way to the rolltop desk.

Working on her project proposal would set her head straight. She always found excitement when it came to framing up an idea on the screen. On the trip down here, she'd thought about several design elements she wanted to implement in her proposed design, but she could only keep her attention for so long—too many thoughts and distractions had set her off course. Sitting behind a screen, even at two in the morning, would give her a focus, a chance to pour out all her ideas and a creative outlet that always led to a restful sleep.

After about an hour of work, Molly had the satisfaction of droopy lids. She carefully ignored the whispers of worry for tomorrow as she powered down her computer. Instead of climbing upstairs and risking her mind revving up again, she snuggled up on the old corduroy couch and dragged the quilt off the back to cover up. Before allowing herself to drift off, she whispered out her worries and muttered a little prayer. "Give me strength. Let this be about Grandad. Not about me."

* * *

The next morning, Jack bounded up the porch steps, trying to concentrate on his surroundings more than his thoughts. A stubborn woodpecker kept his ears busy, and the slight drizzle had him rush beneath the porch overhang. Running his fingers through his hair to distribute the raindrops, he made a mental note to check the forecast, as any decent farmer should, but his mind had been foggy today.

Jack's quick knock mimicked the woodpecker's rhythm, but the sharp click of heels approaching from the other side threw off any harmonizing.

The door swung open, and Molly appeared. Her eyes were softer than yesterday. She seemed to resemble the girl he once knew. Maybe it was the all-black attire but, although similar to her fashion back then, he didn't recall any high-school girl wearing a sophisticated dress like that. Her curves were just slightly obvious before the skirt flared out and hit just above the knee.

He ran his finger between his neck and collar, trying to figure out what to say after *good morning*.

Molly's lips parted, little color but lots of shine. He realized she was wearing hardly any makeup.

"Hey there. You want to come inside?" Even her voice was more natural, just plain words without any sarcasm or surprise—or anything, really. Said just what they meant. Tone may have been washed away with sorrow today.

"Sure." He stepped into Gertie's living room and wiped his boots on the floor mat. He fumbled with his phone. "I'm going to check the forecast. You might want to grab a couple umbrellas."

"Good idea. Don't let me forget. I'm going to check

on Gran first." Molly clicked past the stairs and slipped into Gertie's downstairs bedroom. Jack focused on the screen—or tried to. He was still taken aback by Molly's appearance. Yesterday, she was as sharp as the shadows of a noontime sun. But today? Not one feature appeared sharp. Only soft. She seemed fragile but grounded. Not overly bright, but not completely subdued. The perfect picture of pretty. Yes, Molly Jansen was the prettiest lady he'd seen in a long while.

A muffled sob escaped from Gran's room. *Pretty* was a word that seemed petty in this moment. A cloud skipped right out of the sky and flooded the space beneath the Austin roof. Jack's muscles tensed. He put his phone in his pocket and sat on the bench, lowering his head to pray.

So much peace needed this day. A widow was saying goodbye to the love of her life. Fifty years of loving. Jack had only loved like that for six years of his own life, and his heart was tangled up like corn silk in his chest.

When the women emerged from the room, Gertie leaned into Molly as if she would crumple to the ground at the slightest separation.

"Hey there, Jack." Gertie wore sunglasses, but the dipping corners of her mouth gave away the mourning those glasses tried to conceal. "It's about that time..." Her lips quivered, and she shoved a handkerchief in her face. "Oh, I don't know that I can do this."

Molly wrapped her arm around her shoulders in a full-on hug. "You can, Gran. I'll be right here."

Gertie pulled off her sunglasses. Every crease and wrinkle were deepened by the grief sewn on her face. "How can we go on with this? Without...without... Annie?"

Molly's expression suddenly froze to ice. Jack rose, feeling the need to step between the two.

"Gran, I thought you'd come to peace with that." Molly's words cut the air like paper slicing the very thinnest layer of skin.

"Most days."

"Well, this day is going on as planned. There's nothing to be done about Mom."

"She received my letter."

Molly's face blanched. She stepped back. "What?"

Gertie broke away from her granddaughter and gripped the back of the couch. "We found her. Didn't we, Jack?"

Molly glared his way. He rubbed his hands together. "We…we did. But it's not good, Mol."

"Please don't call me that." Molly folded her arms across her chest. Memories began to flood him now. A flash of anger dissolved the last of her softness from earlier. "Where is she?"

Jack exchanged glances with Gertie, who nodded. He had not expected to be part of this conversation. But the pain in Gertie's eyes and the hurt in Molly's increased his desire to be strong—a certain strength Rob had possessed in Jack's time of need. Jack spoke low and steady, like when he tried to distract Tate during his breathing treatments. "She's in a penitentiary in California."

Molly released her arms and lowered to sit on the stairs. She shook her head. "Did she write back?"

Gertie replied, "No. But I sent the letter by registered mail. Jack checked the website. We know the jail received it. But she never wrote back."

"How long ago?"

"The day of the accident. About a month ago."

Both women stared down at their hands. The cloud turned into a near-palpable heaviness in the old house. No words were uttered. Jack wondered if anyone breathed. He spied the umbrellas hanging on a hook in the mudroom down the hall to the kitchen. He left the two women and retrieved the umbrellas, figuring it was the best way to tell them they needed to leave soon.

When he returned, Molly blocked him at the living-room entrance. "Who have you told?" she demanded.

"What?"

"Who am I going to face that will ask questions about her?" Her nose was pink, her eyelids pressing against a wave of tears.

"Molly, you have nothing to worry about." He placed both umbrellas in one hand and tried to wrap his arm around her.

His comfort was quickly discarded by a firm push. "Thanks, Jack. But you really can't understand all I've had to worry about." She wiped at her eyes with the backs of her fingers and walked away. Grabbing a small purse from the armchair, she called out, "I'll be in the truck." Molly sailed out of the house, leaving the front door ajar but the screen door slamming shut.

Gertie rummaged through her purse on the console table behind the couch. "Where did I put that?" she mumbled breathlessly. Her hands moved about frantically, and she whimpered.

"Hey, Gertie, what are you looking for?" Jack approached and cupped her elbow.

She pushed her sunglasses farther up her nose. "I just want a piece of gum." Her shoulders slumped, as if she'd lost a battle with gum.

"Don't worry." He released her elbow and pulled a roll of mints out of his front pocket.

"Thank you." She took a mint with trembling fingers.

"Hard to see anything with those glasses, no doubt," he said gently teasing, desperate to lower the tension.

She swatted at him playfully. No smile, but a quiet reply. "Funny guy."

Jack offered her his arm. She slipped her hand through, and he escorted her to the door.

Gertie paused as they reached the shaft of light tumbling across the old wood floors from the doorway. "I shouldn't have said anything to Molly."

"Probably not the best time."

"Yesterday was a better day for me. I was able to see things straight. Today, everything's topsy-turvy."

"To be expected." Jack squeezed her hand resting in the crook of his arm.

When they stepped onto the porch, he caught a glimpse of Molly in the back seat of the truck. She glanced his way without expression, then faced forward.

"She'll warm up." Gertie sniffled. "Once I apologize. Poor girl will never get what she wants."

"What's that?" Jack grimaced as they carefully walked down the steps.

"A wound all stitched up."

Jack had arrived here trying to focus on anything but the man they would bury today. But now, he welcomed the chance to reflect on the life of Rob Austin. His family had suffered much, were still suffering from old and new wounds. Jack felt like he could honor Rob most by being there for those the man had left behind, even if he was pushed away in his effort.

Chapter Four

By the time they pulled up to the church, the rain had stopped and the sun promised to heat up the humid air as it broke free from the clouds. Molly opened her own door before Jack had the chance to offer, and she waited on the sidewalk flanking a flower bed of daffodils along the brick fellowship hall. Jack assisted Gran, offering his elbow like he had back at the farmhouse.

Molly walked on the other side of Gran as they climbed the church steps. She swallowed hard and clenched her teeth, forcing herself to close the gap between her and Gertie by slipping her hand in the crook of Gran's arm.

Quiet sobs lifted Gran's shoulders, and the hearse parked along the road sobered Molly to this present moment. Devastation at the withheld news about Mom would just have to wait. Molly needed to hold onto Gran as much as the frail woman needed help in keeping steady.

The tall stands of lilies on either side of the sanctuary door masked the musty scent of her childhood church. Short brown pews, a red runner down the center aisle

and the art-deco stained glass of a cross and a dove in
the window above the altar were all the same as she remembered.

Molly slid her eyes to the few people sitting in the
pews but noticed the casket just to the right of the lec-
tern. Her own silent weeping flooded her chest and wobbled her stomach, and she spent the rest of the service
trying to manage her composure.

When Jack gave the eulogy, Molly forced herself to
listen even though she felt like crossing her arms and
looking away. Molly wasn't sure if Jack should be up
there now. She paid attention only because this was for
her grandfather. But Jack honored Grandad in such a
way that Molly's inner monologue began to crumble. A
fresh wave of tears brewed. She was almost convinced
that Jack deserved to speak about him.

At the end of the service, anxiety pinched between her
shoulder blades as she and Gran received condolences
from everyone. Molly wasn't sure that she breathed at
all. Several of the folks were farmers in the area, men
and women who had come over for the Austins' annual
barbecue when Molly was little. They only commented
on how much she had grown and how impressed they
were with her architecture success. Gran had been right:
Grandad must have bragged big, because even amid the
grief, these folks saw her as a celebrity.

Molly finally let out a long sigh after the last person
squeezed her hands and shuffled down the narrow cor-
ridor to the fellowship hall for the reception Her high-
school classmates were probably too busy with kids and
their own schedules on a Saturday to stop by the church.
Not that she could blame them, and honestly, she was
thankful not to face them.

Gran's sister, Lola, came up and wrapped her arm around Gertie. Her face was more oval than Gran's heart-shaped face, and although the woman was older by three years, she donned a young hairstyle: soft blond hair dyed to perfection and curled with an obvious hairspray sheen.

Lola spoke softly. "Gertie, I am thinking you aren't very hungry?"

"No, I am not."

"I wasn't able to eat a bite at my George's funeral." She flashed a knowing look at Molly and winked. "So I have a pot of tea ready for us by the office armchairs."

"Shouldn't I be with everyone?" Gran's face hardly changed expression. She wore the same wearied look through the entire service and during the receiving line.

"Who says so?" Lola asked. "You're in charge here."

"Sounds like *you* are," Gran quipped on a half laugh, and the two women tromped ahead, turning into the office instead of heading toward the buffet line that neared the hall doorway.

"Seems like Lola is a good sister." Jack spoke over Molly's shoulder. She hadn't realized he was there.

"She always brings a little joy to the room." Molly tucked her hair behind her ear. Jack stepped beside her. "They will have fun together when she moves to West Des Moines."

Jack adjusted his black tie at the center of his starched white button-down shirt. His tanned jawline flinched. He opened his mouth as if to speak but just cleared his throat and narrowed his eyes toward the dwindling buffet line.

Last time he'd hinted at his resistance to Gran selling the farm, Molly hadn't known his situation. He was a father, a widower and apparently Grandad's closest colleague. She fought a niggle of regret for mentioning Gran's exodus thirty miles away and stared straight ahead. After passing the little church office where the women were balancing teacups on their chair arms, Molly couldn't help but smile as the excitable lilt of whatever story Lola was sharing with Gran traveled down the hall behind them all the way to the reception.

In the fellowship hall, a county-sized feast spread along rectangular tables covered with blue-and-white checked tablecloths. Besides pinwheels of turkey and cream cheese, all sorts of egg bakes, potato casseroles and variations of macaroni and cheese marched along in glass dishes and aluminum-foil pans. All the savory food was followed by scotcharoos, lemon bars and a whole bunch of Dutch pastries. If there was one thing a Midwest church function was known for, it was the plethora of casseroles and desserts.

Tapping a plastic plate against her fist, Molly opted for salad and a pinwheel, then gave in to her sweet tooth and placed a Dutch letter on her napkin. She could never pass up the *S*-shaped pastry with almond paste and crystalized sugar.

She grabbed an iced tea and turned to scan the room for a seat.

"Want to sit outside?" Jake suggested. Molly glanced out the window to the playground. A gazebo and picnic table had been added after her time of scaling the monkey bars and spinning the merry-go-round.

"Sure," she said and followed him out the glass door. "Oh man, it's like an oven out here."

"Should be okay in the shade," Jack called over his shoulder. "There's a breeze."

Molly was doubtful but sweating a little seemed worth not having to make small talk with near strangers who'd last seen her when she was only waist-high to most of them.

Jack sat across from Molly beneath the hexagonal gazebo roof. He had tried to avoid her gaze while he gave the eulogy today. In his peripheral vision he could see her shoulders shaking. How could he possibly assure her that everything would be all right after this morning? Of course, having her ex there on such a fragile day wasn't ideal, but then finding out the guy she hadn't seen in over a decade knew a family secret, that she wasn't even aware of? That was definitely a rotten blow.

Now that Gertie was being cared for by her sister, Jack hoped he could at least give Molly a chance to see him in a different light. To know that of all the folks in Polk Center, he was trustworthy. Rob had taught him the importance of that. And Jack felt just as obligated to care for Rob's granddaughter as he did for his widow. Even if Jack wasn't much of a shoulder to lean on when Molly had needed it most, he'd at least make that up to her before she headed back to the city.

"It's been a while since I've loaded my plate at a church function." She widened her eyes glancing down at her plate.

"That's hardly loaded." Jack lifted his eyebrows and tilted his very full plate toward her. They both laughed.

"Well, it's been a while. For me."

"I bet. Sounds like you've kept yourself busy." Jack steadied his gaze on his food. "Rob would talk and talk about you—"

She snickered. "Wish I was a fly on the wall at my

grandparents' house…" Her smile faded. "Guess he was right about one thing. I kept myself busy." Molly looked about the yard. Her makeupless eyes were bright and soft. Straight teeth rested on her glossy lip as she studied the *L*-shaped church building framing the yard to their left. "But I hope to achieve whatever honors they've already given me."

"What's it like?" Jack put his fork down, rested his hands on the table between his torso and his plate and offered all his attention to her.

"What?"

"Being a big-shot architect?" He grinned wide. Her lips parted, but instead of replying, Molly lowered her gaze to her ranch-drenched lettuce. "Come on, Mol… I mean, Molly. I am honestly interested."

Swallowing her food, she set her fork down. "Look, you know enough about me. I am just thankful you suggested we eat out here so I could get away from small talk."

He chuckled and shook his head. "Thing is, I would like to talk about anything unrelated to this day." He shifted his gaze just past her to the sunflowers lining the chain-link fence at the edge of the yard. "Thought it might help you too."

Molly picked up her fork again and pushed around her salad. "If you consider drawing the complicated plans of a superstore in an Illinois suburb big-shot worthy, then I guess I deserve a pat on the back." She returned a smile before her next bite.

"No way." Jack leaned back, then forward again. He set his arms on the table and rested his chest on his forearms. "Your Grandad said you helped with loft apartments downtown."

"Uh, I did…kinda. I took the senior architect's first attempt at technical drawings and inputted his redlines." She tucked her hair behind her ear and cast a simmering look his way. "You gotta do the grunt work to get to the good stuff, though." Molly winked. Any trace of a smile Jack could manage was gone. Her words lurched his heart forward. "I suppose if you were around Grandad as much as you said you were, you'd have heard that bit of advice."

He nodded. "Yes, ma'am. I've heard that plenty of times. Even use it myself when I'm around the detasseling crew."

Molly groaned and rolled her eyes. "Ugh! That's exactly what I think when I hear the phrase *grunt work*—yanking those tassels on the top of the corn plants." She nibbled on her sandwich. "But the second thing I think of is sitting at a desk till late at night…working on someone else's masterpiece." That last word began with a twinkle in her blue eyes and ended on a sigh. Molly was a dreamer. He remembered that. They'd sit on the old porch swing and talk about their dreams after high school. All he could remember was his. He wondered if he'd ever listened to her or if she'd had any dreams of her own back then.

He tilted his head and asked, "So how close are you to the good stuff?"

"Ah, I can almost taste it." Determination dripped from each syllable. "My chance is sitting on my laptop, and I hope to win over the senior staff at my firm." She set her fork down again as she described a high-end residence with glass and solar panels and a killer atrium. Her hands were necessary to illustrate the roof pitch and the orientation of the Mississippi to the property line.

Jack laughed when she finally punctuated the air where the cutting-edge light fixture might go. "You are like my little guy on Christmas morning." He leaned close enough to appraise the exact number of freckles dusting her nose. He'd not try, because he really wanted her to hear his next words. "That's why Rob bragged about you."

She shifted in her seat. The corners of her mouth tugged down. "What do you mean?"

"Your passion to be part of something bigger than yourself. He always said that you were changing the Chicago skyline with the heart of a farmer."

Molly's blue eyes filled, and she looked away.

"Most days I forget that farming is about being part of something bigger than yourself." Jack gave her room, pulled away, clutching the edge of the picnic table. "It's why I got into it in the first place. Nothing like it... except being a parent, I guess."

Molly continued to look away, swiping her eyes with her finger. He gave her a moment and continued eating. She broke off the end of her Dutch letter and ate slowly.

Fatigue hit him—all the pent-up emotion of the morning was settling heavily in his chest. The pressure had been nearly constant the few months after Brittany passed. Afterward, relief only came in short spurts until that next trigger sent him down a spiral of memories or the awareness of being slightly less than adequate for Tate. He didn't mean to turn the attention back to himself. But now, he'd dug himself into his own deep well of mourning and couldn't think of what to say next.

Molly brushed crumbs off her lap and asked, "How old is your son?"

Jack ran his hand through his hair, thankful she was

stepping into his world when he just couldn't manage to get out of his own head. "Four. Full of energy. And a personality to love. He sure makes life interesting."

"That's a lot to juggle, a farm and a kid. I won't even get a pet goldfish right now." She giggled.

Jack lifted his shoulders and swallowed past all the aching in his throat. "It's definitely been a lot to manage." He sighed. "Brittany made it look easy."

Molly pushed her chin up and said, "I am so sorry, Jack."

He exhaled deeply. "If I am honest, it's been pretty hard. I suggest you don't get a pet."

"Not planning on it." She widened her eyes and pursed her lips together in jest.

Jack thrummed his fingers on the table. His ring's tan line was still obvious on his finger. He'd only taken it off at the beginning of this summer. Mostly because it wasn't smart to work around machinery with any chance of the ring catching on it.

A few clouds gathered just beyond the roofline of the gazebo, casting shade on the sunflowers. "I feel like I am coming up short more than anything." He clicked his tongue like Rob used to when he couldn't put a finger on what he was trying to say. "There's just some things a mother does best for a kid…" He heard his words after he said them, mainly because they manifested themselves in a wave of hurt across Molly's brow. "Oh, I didn't mean to—"

Her lips hardened into a curt smile, and she piled her fork and her napkin on top of her unfinished plate. "I get it. Really, I do." She took a drink of her tea. "I better go check on Gran."

Jack swung his legs around the bench and stood.

Molly was already to her feet and had her plate in her hands. "Molly, is there anything I can do?"

"Mind opening the door?" She said the words like he was insensitively standing by while she was moving a heavy piece of equipment. He was certain that even if her arms weren't bearing much weight, her heart was, and he had gone and made it worse by mentioning the things a mother does best for their children to a woman whose mother had given everything but her best.

Chapter Five

Molly and Gran simultaneously sighed when they walked into the living room after Lola dropped them off that afternoon. While golden sunrays cut large swaths across the room, Molly felt as though the day had dragged on into the night, and all she wanted to do was sleep.

"I think I am going to lie down." Gran took the words right out of her mouth.

"Me too." Molly began up the stairs while Gran slipped her shoes off and slid them under the bench by the front door. Molly turned around to ask her if she needed anything, but Gran had already disappeared into her room.

Molly changed into her Notre Dame T-shirt and cotton pajama bottoms. She slipped under the covers and closed her eyes. A decade had passed, yet the quiet house begged for the rich voice of Grandad. He'd often come home from church, change into comfortable clothes and turn on a game. Molly shuddered. He wasn't coming home. A tear rolled down her cheek as she recalled the sterile hospital room and his raspy, "See you soon". Her eyes opened, and she blinked away residual moisture. She thought about Jack's eulogy. He mentioned Grandad's work ethic, his joy, his wisdom. Jack's words were spot on. Her stomach twisted as she considered their conversation outside.

She hadn't expected the girl she had been in Polk Center to compete with the woman she was now. But sitting at her childhood church while Jack talked about the importance of a mother, Molly was reminded of all she'd lacked without Mom in her life. Grief clattered so recklessly within her. She had no idea what the things were that a mother did best. And Molly would not venture backward in her mind to try and scrape the barrel of Mom's good traits. The woman was now in jail without a word, Molly had moved on and Jack knew way too much. She could politely excuse herself anywhere else if something triggered her emotion. Not here. Not in Polk Center. Jack knew her wounds, and she would always be the daughter of a woman whose addictions had caused deep embarrassment and lasting scars.

She flung back the covers and decided it was never too early to get started on her next priority: sell this house. Molly was an adult with big plans. This was an unpleasant detour along the way. This was the grunt work to get to the good stuff. And unlike her work back at the firm, she was the one in charge of how fast this work could go. Might as well get started. She headed downstairs, grabbed the half-eaten Dutch letter wrapped in a napkin in her purse and headed to the kitchen.

Gran still had an old rotary phone hanging on the wall. Molly picked it up. No dial tone. She expected the faint scent of Grandad's aftershave on the receiver like when she was younger. But it probably hadn't been used in years. She sighed and hung up. It truly was a decorative antique. Moving the cord away from the drawer beneath it, she pulled out a pad and pen.

"First things first," she said aloud as she wrote *To Do* on the first line of the yellow paper.

Walls.

They didn't have time to knock any down and open up the floorplan, but they could at least strip them of the decades-old wallpaper and cover up any blemishes with a fresh coat of paint. She glanced about at the peeling papered corners just beneath the faded oak trim. So much life lived while that glue was losing its stickiness.

Molly sighed and jotted down *Buy scraper and texture*.

Molly didn't love the idea of taking shortcuts when she'd been trained to care about the bones of a place. Maybe she should just dip into the giant savings her dad had gifted her from his inheritance and hire a crew to do the job properly. She feared spending too much time on the walls of this place would inevitably lead to crumbling the walls around her heart. The work of tearing down one would inevitably expose the other. Today had tested those walls, and she was pretty sure they could not handle any type of exposure right now.

The sound of an engine roared above the clanky window air-conditioning unit behind her. She leaped up from her chair just as the engine cut off. Peeking over the unit, the air blowing at her midsection, Jack emerged from his truck, shut the door and headed around the corner toward the kitchen door.

"Cooling off?" Gran startled her. She swiveled with her pad and pen to her chest.

"Oh, yep. But now I am cold." Molly laughed nervously and rushed past her. "Going to run up and get my sweatshirt."

"Sweatshirt? That old wall unit hardly blows cold air." Gran patted her shoulder. "Let's have some iced tea—"

A knock rapped on the door.

"Um, no. I think I'd like to try and sleep again. Couldn't catch a wink before." Molly hurried across the living-room floor.

Gran called out, "Molly, we have a visitor, though."

"You have a good visit. I'll be down before dinner." Molly took the stairs two at a time, hitting every creaky spot on the way up.

Jack's low voice carried through the house. The walls were just too thin to completely ignore their visitor. Molly fell back on her bed and let the pen and paper drop to the floor.

She unplugged her phone from the charger and opened the app to her online banking. Her nest egg was a nice cushion for that condo she had been planning since she first moved to Chicago. The inheritance money was the icing on all her hard work to keep going and learning and creating. How much of her savings could she part with to pay for professionals to remodel this house if it meant she could head out of Polk Center ASAP?

Her door creaked open with a quick knock. Gran appeared, her eyes puffy but her lips offering an assuring smile. "Jack wanted to check on you. Said you all had a tense moment back at lunch. Sure you don't want to come down?"

Molly set her phone on the nightstand and scooted up. "Not right now, Gran. This is all just too much." Her throat squeezed with emotion.

Gran nodded, and her smile turned to a frown. "For

all of us, dear. But we have much work to do. Tomorrow is a new day, right?"

How Molly wished tomorrow would kick up dust in her rearview mirror, leaving this place behind. For good? A twist in her chest only provoked bittersweetness. No relief.

"Yeah, let's give it a night and sleep on it. Then tomorrow will be full steam ahead." Molly picked up her pen and pad. "I've already gotten started." She winked at Gran. "You know what Ms. Leigh says about tomorrow." Of course she did. Gran had first introduced Molly to *Gone with the Wind* during a late-night movie marathon while they waited for Grandad during harvest.

Gran softly chuckled and closed the door.

Molly just couldn't leave Gran with a crew to do all the grunt work. This wasn't just hard for Molly, like her grandmother had said.

Molly would just have to spend the night reinforcing her own walls to get to work on these old ones.

The next morning, Jack scooped Tate out of bed, got him situated in his medical vest in front of the television and plugged in his nebulizer. As always, Tate hummed loudly over the motor while the vest shook his voice as if he were riding a tractor over muddy row beds.

Jack chuckled as he sipped his coffee. Only his playful Tate could bring joy from the serious equipment used to break up the mucus in his lungs.

"How about we head to the Polk Center bakery for doughnuts after this episode?" Jack spoke loudly over the vest, nebulizer and blaring cartoons.

Tate gave two thumbs-up and smiled beneath his transparent mask.

Jack headed to his room and got ready for a day at the farm. But instead of spending his Saturday in the sunshine, he'd spend it inside. After an overwhelmed Gertie had assured him that she would put in a good word for Jack's future employment to any buyer, she had also asked him to come by and fix her bathroom sink and various other projects around the place today. He'd hoped to smooth things over with Molly too. She hadn't been up for his visit yesterday, and although he'd played it as if he was just checking in on both women, he had stopped by after the funeral to apologize to Molly for upsetting her.

Today was hopefully a fresh start. Jack peeked out the blinds next to his bathroom sink. Not one cloud in the sky but plenty of rain in the ground to keep those crops growing. Showing up to help, with entertaining Tate and a box full of doughnuts, would bring a little needed sunshine in Rob's absence.

After packing Tate's backpack with books, toy tractors and his digestive enzymes, Jack wrestled with the little guy to get him to change out of his pajamas and into actual clothes.

"Miss Gertie has a guest at her house. First impressions, bud."

"Dad, what's cooler than a superhero?" Tate clenched his pajama shirt as Jack tried to lift it over his head.

Jack stepped back and couldn't figure out how to reason with Tate. Brittany had had a way about her when it came to dealing with their child. Jack figured her sweet demeanor had charmed their son as much as it had him. Now he only felt frustration at his lack of charm or patience with his son.

"Look, we'll just skip doughnuts." Jack tossed the

T-shirt and jeans on Tate's unmade bed. "I need you to obey."

Tate whined, "But Daddy! We haven't had doughnuts in a million years."

"Last Saturday. And the one before that. Tate, all I am asking is for you to get dressed." Jack shoved his hands in his pockets and swiveled around. "You've got five minutes."

He crossed through the living room, stepping over socks and trains, and ran his hands through his hair. Disappointment filled his chest as he once again caught the beautiful day outside. He was tired of the struggle that constantly dredged up how good they once had it, and how something missing would forever cloud their moments. Sure, Jack knew kids would test their parents. He'd done his fair share of that with his own. But how could he let these episodes pass by without crashing into what once was and would never be again?

Seems like he had done the same thing to Molly yesterday. Their conversation had taken a turn to her never-was-before and never-will-be.

"Come on, Tate," Jack called. "Let's just go—"

"I'm ready!" He jogged down the hall with his jeans unbuttoned and his shirt bunched up just above his rounded belly. "But I can't button these, Daddy. Can you do it?"

Jack smiled and crouched down to help. "Thanks for listening to me, bud. We've just got to work together."

"So can I get two doughnuts?" Tate raised an eyebrow and tilted his head as if bracing himself to take advantage of the situation.

Jack ruffled his hair, then stood. "Maybe. But you

need to help me pick out what to get for Miss Gertie and her granddaughter, Molly."

"Molly? How old is she?"

"My age."

"Oh!" He guffawed and dropped his shoulders. "I guess just plain. That's what you grown-ups like." He rolled his eyes, then ran across the floor, grabbing his sneakers by the back door.

Jack chuckled, whispering a quick prayer of thanks for this tiny moment of redemption. Although, he also prayed for parenting skills that didn't require dough-nuts as bribes.

Chapter Six

Molly sat on the old porch swing with her laptop and a coffee mug. One thing she loved about being back in the country was the quiet. No crazy traffic, sirens or horns blaring outside her picture window. No cool breeze gently scented with exhaust floating along her narrow balcony. She inhaled deeply. Dew in the air, rustles of cottonwoods along the property's perimeter and her laptop connecting her to everything she hoped for in the city—

Wait.

Molly slid her finger back and forth on the touchpad. Her cursor froze over her 3D model on the screen. She took a deep breath and diverted her eyes to the screen door. The scent of freshly brewed coffee met her nostrils. Across the living room at the entrance to the kitchen, Gran's silhouette was framed by the sunny kitchen window. She held a newspaper.

Molly had saved her progress continuously, so there was no reason to panic. Trying one more time with a tap of her finger, she decided to close it up for now and join Gran.

"Good morning," she called as she walked across the creaky living-room floor. "I have a list chock-full of items to get done today."

Gran put the paper down and smiled as Molly passed behind her. "That's good, dear. But coffee first."

"Absolutely," Molly said as she dumped out her cold coffee in the sink. "I am sorry I didn't say good-night last night. I conked out early."

"Oh, me too. How long have you been up?"

"Since six. I needed to get a head start on work today. Had some ideas I wanted to implement." Molly filled her cup and joined Gran at the table. "Maybe we can go to Longfellow's home improvement store after church?"

Gran shrugged her shoulders. "I might just go to the evening service. It's a little less crowded."

"Sure." By the worry in Gran's pale eyes, Molly could only imagine she was replaying yesterday's funeral. At least, that was what immediately formed in Molly's mind at the mention of church. "It's okay to take some time, Gran. Everyone will understand." She patted her hand but wondered when she decided this was good advice. Molly had never taken it herself, thinking that her absence would only make people talk more. At least when she showed up in the pew, most people didn't have the audacity to talk about her. School had been a different story, though. Molly sighed. "Let's head to the store after breakfast, then. Most of the little jobs just require light bulbs and new hardware. We can also look at paint colors. I am thinking the bathrooms and this kitchen—"

"Oh my," Gran exclaimed and sat back with sigh. "This is going to be quite an undertaking."

"Don't worry. You can do as much or as little as you like."

Gran looked around the place. "How long before we list it?"

"Well, calling a real estate agent is at the top of my list. I looked up numbers this morning before working. We'll call them first thing tomorrow."

A knock startled them both. Molly looked at the clock on the microwave: 8:09. "Who's here so early on a Sunday?"

Gran stood and crossed over to the door. "It's Jack."

Molly gulped her coffee, burning her throat. She took a deep breath reminding herself that the only thing that mattered was getting this house ready. Whatever Jack thought of her, or knew about her, would not get this house sold any quicker or her project finished for the presentation. He was only a distraction.

Gran opened the door, and Jack stepped inside. His hair was wet and combed neatly, but his five-o'clock shadow matched the casual look of his ripped jeans and an old T-shirt with a stretched-out collar. No need to impress. Good. She didn't need impressing.

He caught her eye, nodded and smiled. Okay, well, the smile outdressed everyone in the room. "Good morning." He held up a toolbox in salutation.

"Morning," she managed to say, diverting her eyes to her coffee. Well, maybe he could at least be a useful distraction.

"You brought a helper," Gran exclaimed and widened the door. A little boy appeared with a big box of doughnuts in his arms and a dinosaur backpack over his shoulders.

"He insisted on carrying them." Jack bent down and guided his son to the table. "Here we go." He put the box in front of Molly. The little boy looked like Jack with the same combed hair, only darker, and a genuine smile. His freckles and baby blues were all his own.

"This must be Tate." Molly stood and gathered her laptop and coffee in her hands.

"And you must be Miss Molly," Tate said and held his hand out to her.

Gran cooed as if impressed.

Molly set her mug down and shook the little guy's hand. "Yes, I am. You are quite the gentleman."

"I am a superhero." He lifted his shirt to expose a superhero pajama shirt, then looked up at his father with a mischievous grin.

Jack ran his hand through his hair and chuckled softly. "Wise guy."

Tate took his backpack off and hung it on the back of a chair. "Can we eat now?"

Gran hurried over, gave Tate a squeeze around the shoulders, then opened the box. "Let's see, I guess those sprinkle ones are for you, Tate?" She grabbed a napkin from the basket and set it in front of the boy.

"Yes, ma'am." He did a little dance move in his seat and rubbed his hands together as Gran set the doughnut down.

"Hold up," Jack said and unzipped the backpack. "You need your beads, son." He pulled out a giant medical bottle, opened it and handed Tate a massive pill. The little boy opened the capsule and poured little beads into his mouth, swallowed them audibly, then began to dig into his doughnut. Jack leaned over and said to Molly, "He has digestive stuff. Part of dealing with cystic fibrosis. Those help him break down the food."

"Oh, I see." Molly gave a weak smile, surprised that the energetic boy had a chronic illness. Gran sat across from Tate and began to ask him about preschool while Jack helped himself to coffee. This quiet morning was suddenly crowded, and Molly felt like the stranger. She slipped out of the room and set her laptop on the desk, deciding she would check to see if it worked again.

"Hey, everything okay?" Jack leaned on the entryway trim, his mug in his hands.

"Um, yeah." Molly tried the trackpad again. Phew, it worked. She stuck her fist on her hip and faced him. "We have loads to do around here. What are you up to today?"

His questioning look, arched eyebrows and clenched teeth barely showing from parting lips were an unspoken reminder of their last conversation.

"Look, there is nothing else to be said. We just have to focus on this place. And I have to get back to Chicago as soon as we do. If you and...Tate are here for breakfast, then we better eat. Gran and I are heading to the store straight after." She did not want to have any emotional discussions or dredge up any past communications. Today was the start of her exit out of Polk Center.

Jack lifted a hand in surrender. "Sounds good to me. But Tate and I are here to help. Well, I am, anyway. Tate might just hang from the rafters." That dimple appeared, volleying his charm to that sparkle in those brown eyes.

Why'd his smile have to be so contagious? She reined in her own by taking a sip of her coffee. She composed herself and said, "I'll get the list, and you can decide what to do." Molly started toward the kitchen, but Jack didn't budge from filling up the doorway with his muscular stature. Sure, the entryway was the width of double doors, but Molly chose to go through the living room to the doorway by the mudroom. The notepad was covered with runaway sprinkles next to a very frosting-covered Tate.

"Looks like you need another napkin." Molly handed him one from the basket.

Gran was at the sink. "He needs more than that." She held up a wash rag and came over to wipe Tate's nose and chin and cheeks. "Was it good?"

"Uh-huh." Tate nodded. Molly shook off her notepad into the doughnut box and swiveled around. "Hey, Miss Molly, we got you a doughnut too."

Molly turned back. She surveyed the doughnuts. It had been a while since she had a Polk Center doughnut.

"Glazed. My favorite." She took a napkin and donut, smiled and left the room.

Jack had followed Molly through the living room, not realizing she was going back to the kitchen. She crashed into him just outside the mudroom door.

"Whoa!" He lifted his coffee away just in time to spill on the wood floor and not Molly's sweetly apple-scented head that came just to his chin.

She pressed her hand to his chest and backed up. "I didn't realize you were there."

"I didn't realize you were going to the kitchen." He looked down at her hand, then at his dripping coffee cup. Molly pulled her hand back quickly and tucked her hair behind her ear, keeping her eyes on the dough-nut stacked on the pad of paper in her other hand. Jack stepped closer. She lifted her gaze up at him. Rounded wonders shining with anticipation. Once again, she wasn't wearing makeup. He held his breath, realizing this moment was just as vulnerable as yesterday's lunch. She seemed to think he'd drawn near for something more than just to get a towel for his coffee. Her teeth rested on her lip, and her cheeks flushed red.

"Don't worry." Jack smiled and held up his cup between them. "Nothing hurt." He winked.

Her whole face changed—her eyes narrowed, the corner of her mouth hooked in a wry smile, and she nodded. "Good. Just don't sneak up on me next time."

"Yes, ma'am." He winked and forced himself to continue into the kitchen for a dish towel.

A series of dings sounded from Molly's phone. "I'll just set the list on the back of the couch. My email is going nuts."

After Gran helped Jack clean up, he left her and Tate at the table with a coloring book and headed to the living room. Molly's back was to him as she sat at her desk, intent on her laptop. He bit into a doughnut and skimmed her list. Unease dislodged his peace once again. Every light to be changed, every tool needed, and every call to be made would push Jack closer to losing this place forever. Security for Tate and their life here in Polk Center depended on the buyer of this place. And while he knew Gertie would do her best to get him hired, everything was truly out of his control.

"Argh!" Molly clutched her hair on both sides of her head, and she pressed her face closer to her screen.

"What's up?" Jack happily left the list and stood behind her.

"The internet connection is messing with me. I was writing an important email, and now I don't know if it was sent or not."

Jack went over and checked the connection next to the TV console. "You've probably used the internet more in one day than the Austins have used it since 2000."

He played around with cords. "I think we should try a new router."

Molly burst out of her seat and stood next to him. "Don't tell me it needs to be ordered." She ran her hand through her straight black hair. Apple blossoms in the heat of summer. A refreshing scent. "I might need to find a coffee shop or bookstore with free Wi-Fi."

"Are you talking about going to Des Moines?"

"Of course. I know there's no place with free Wi-Fi near Polk Center."

"You are right. Although, I think the coffee shop, Sweets 'n' Things, over in Grangewood might have Wi-Fi." He stepped back. "But I am pretty sure we can get a router at Longfellow's."

Molly blew air out and up, lifting fine hairs around her forehead. "Good. We were headed there anyway."

"We were?" Jack offered a half smile in jest.

Molly shifted her blue eyes, narrowing them. Her glint of amusement turned his smile full on.

She opened her mouth to speak, but Gran called out, "You two go to the store. I can stay and hang out with Tate. He's teaching me all about superpowers."

Jack nodded. "Sounds about right."

Molly hooked her finger on her chin and stared at her screen, perhaps contemplating the wisdom of an outing with him.

Taking a break from everything that reminded him of Rob and his unknown future would be good for him. And adult conversation on the weekend was a rare bonus. "Promise I know the way." Jack nudged her with his elbow.

Molly gave him a surprised look and cocked her head. "Really?"

"What?" His heart sped up, worrying that she was going to try and rehash everything from yesterday. "I really didn't—"

"You don't remember, do you?" This time, Molly gave him a crooked smile. Tiny dimples dotted her petite chin. "You said those exact words on our way to Alfonso's for homecoming and we got stuck at a train clear on the other side of town."

Oh man, Jack had totally forgotten that, but now he remembered that *Promise I know the way* had become an inside joke every time she got in his truck after homecoming. He chuckled. "I'd say that Chicago-style pizza and Dr. Pepper were just as good as Alfonso's."

"Wow, you remember what we ate." She pursed her lips and offered an affirming nod. "I am impressed."

"That was a great night, Mol." He watched her face soften. Flecks of blue and gold shone bright in the morning sun. A lifetime stretched from this moment all the way back to the moment when Molly Jansen had captured his heart with her quiet confidence and snarky humor. Now her own lifetime shaped this woman who was not so quietly confident but who shared the same memories laced with the same humor and the same radiant beauty.

She stepped back and reached over to close her laptop. Clearing her throat she said, "I'll go get ready." Molly crossed the room quickly and ran upstairs.

"I'll grab the list." He jogged over to the couch and tore off the sheet from the pad then folded it and placed it in his pocket.

Why did he feel like somehow he'd jumped all the way back to the quarterback standing in the middle of his girlfriend's living room? He nearly looked in the mirror by the front door to make sure some time warp hadn't just happened.

He brushed past Molly's desk and saw her sketches on a pad of paper—crisp straight lines, smooth shadows, and abstract plant material bordering building walls. He admired the design, even if it was only on a notepad with notes in block handwriting all over. At least he knew that Molly was no longer the girl who dated the quarterback. She was all grown-up and establishing her career and her own dream. He brushed his finger over the American Institute of Architects sticker on the back of her laptop. No wonder she was ready to knock out this old farmhouse.

Jack looked around the place that had barely changed since he'd last seen Molly in tears on the front steps. He was thankful she'd found her way without him.

She had succeeded. Now she had even bigger and better plans ahead.

While he would not trade one second of the lifetime that filled in this gap between quarterback and farming father, Molly was an inspiration in her determination. At least he could help someone achieve something great right now. Even if it meant replacing an old router and making a mediocre internet connection secure.

Chapter Seven

Molly threw on a T-shirt and shorts, gathered her hair into a ponytail, brushed her teeth, then put on some mascara and lip gloss. No need for a full face today. Even with Jack Behrens downstairs. Especially with Jack downstairs. All the butterflies he stirred up before nine o'clock in the morning were a test. Had Molly grown up or not? She would not cave to her attention to detail for Jack's sake. Her freckles would not be covered with foundation, her cheeks would not be defined with blush, and she certainly wouldn't highlight the gold in her eyes with the pretty eyeshadow her neighbor in Chicago had encouraged her to buy recently.

Nope.

Molly checked the mirror one more time before shutting off the bathroom light. She was pleased with her simple appearance.

She galloped down the stairs. "Ready to go—" She stopped at the last stair, placing her hand on the post without the newel cap.

Gran was at the TV flipping through the channels manually. No sign of Jack or Tate.

"Oh, did they decide to leave?" Molly's voice was higher-pitched than normal. She rolled her eyes at herself. Nope, she did not care if Jack stayed or left. Well, that was not entirely true. "I mean, I really need that part to get my email sent. But I guess—"

"Here we go, superhero." Jack bounded out from the kitchen with Tate on his back. The little boy's arms were above his head like he was about to launch into the air. Jack released Tate into the recliner, then turned to him and began to coach him on being good for Gran.

"I can't seem to find the cartoon station." Gran continued to press the buttons, but most stations were scrambled.

"There's no internet, Gran. Only antenna." Molly grabbed her purse. "Guess Tate's going to have to watch old Westerns like I did at his age."

"Nothing wrong with that," Jack chimed in. Gran shrugged her shoulders and stopped at *Bonanza*. "Any other day, Tate would be dressed in his cowboy boots."

"Good," Gran said. "You two don't worry about us. We have a whole batch of frozen cookie dough to stick in the oven later."

"Wahoo!" Tate shot his fist in the air.

Jack pulled his keys from his pocket and headed past Molly to the front door. "Ready? Got the list." He patted his other pocket as he opened the door.

"Yep." Molly breezed by, catching a glimpse at Grandad's boots on the porch. Life would never be the same without Grandad. At least the sunshine seemed to give permission to take a rest from mourning for a while.

She hurried to the passenger door, before Jack could get it, and scooted into the seat. Cedar and mint simmered in the sun-warmed air, and the dashboard had the usual film of dust that any farm-bound truck collected on the many trips down dirt roads.

Jack slid into his seat. "Sorry for the mess."

"It's fine." She peeked over the seat to the back. A booster seat, crumpled chip bags and Gatorade bottles were littered around the back seat. "Tate is full of energy, huh?"

Jack started the truck, then shifted into Drive. "Oh yeah." They pulled out onto the main road, but instead of turning right to Polk Center they took a left toward the city. "Not a lot of people believe me when they find out he's sick."

"I don't know a thing about cystic fibrosis," Molly admitted.

"It's not good. A lung disease. Basically, he's on the defense all his life, trying to prevent mucus and bacteria from completely taking over his lungs." Jack pulled some sunglasses from his visor and put them on. Molly took out her Ray-Bans from the case in her purse. "All sorts of other issues crop up too. Like his digestive enzymes are out of whack."

"So there's no cure?"

"Nope, just maintaining lung capacity and health. Science has made great strides, though. Only a decade ago, the average life expectancy was in the twenties—"

"What?" Molly whipped her head to him, shocked at the severity of such a disease in his lively little boy. "That's horrible."

"But with the advances in medicine, that can almost double. And some folks have lived well past fifty."

Molly pressed back into her seat. Double? That was still only in the forties. A little over a decade away from Molly's age now. Twelve years. In twelve years, she planned on so much more than she had now. A condo of her own, a chance to be a senior designer, maybe even a family. Maybe. "Forty is young."

"I know. Believe me." Jack sighed. "My wife was really involved in the Cystic Fibrosis Foundation for the first couple years of Tate's life. Even through her chemo. I am so glad she got to see the latest drug hit the market. Tate doesn't qualify for it yet, but man, it does wonders for CF patients."

Molly glanced out the window. The rows of corn zipped by as they drove past, like watching a movie on fast-forward or flipping through one of those old cartoon flipbooks. Cornstalk frames and dirt-path rows, marching along from one to the next. Life went by way too fast. And for Jack and Tate, slowing it down was their constant way of living.

They didn't talk much more on the rest of the twenty-minute trip. Jack turned on the radio and the latest hits took over the conversation.

When they pulled into the store parking lot, Jack took out the list and handed it to Molly. "Seems you should have this more than me."

Molly smiled eagerly and tucked the paper into her purse. "As long as you know which router to get, I don't mind taking care of all of this." She opened her door and hopped down.

Jack jogged around the front of the truck and met up with her as she walked toward the doors. "This must be an architect's favorite place."

"Eh. Maybe. I tend to roam around art-supply stores more that home improvement stores." She slid her sunglasses on top of her head. "I like to draw the plans. The contractor can get all the materials." And the kinds of projects Molly targeted were high-end. "But I do love going to the stone suppliers and custom cabinetry stores to dream the perfect elements to draw up." The same ripple of excitement she'd carried from her first year of studios in college all the way through to this last year of getting noticed for her precision fluttered across her chest. She caught Jack looking at her, his own sunglasses hanging off his collar, and his lips fixed in a half smile without any cockiness or sarcasm. Almost as if in... admiration?

Molly turned her head quickly, and her stomach dropped at such a heady thought. She pressed her hand to her cheek to be sure she wasn't growing beet red as she often did when she was embarrassed.

"Hey there, Jack!" A blonde woman headed toward them pushing a shopping cart with a little girl in pigtails sitting in the front.

"Hi, Chelle." They stopped just as the sliding glass doors opened. Jack stepped aside, and the woman rested her forearms on the handle, as if she would stay a while. Molly didn't recognize her. She stayed back, closest to the door, nearly behind the woman.

"That's just awful about Rob. I know that you were close." The woman fiddled with the little girl's curls. "We were going to come to the funeral, but my sitter fell through."

"It was a nice service." Jack glanced quickly at Molly and back at the woman who didn't once look at Molly, but then again, she might have not realized Molly was with Jack. "We're going to grab some stuff to fix up his house."

Now the woman looked at Molly. "Hi, I am Chelle. Are you a relative of the Austins?" She held out her hand to shake. Molly took it, realizing exactly who stood before her: Rochelle James. The one girl who'd called her Little Lady all through senior year because of Mom running off with the guy referred to as Tramp. Of course Molly didn't need to venture into Polk Center to bump into her past. Everyone shopped in Des Moines.

Now Molly was sure she was beet red as Rochelle narrowed her eyes, as if trying to place her. "Yep. I better go get started." Molly released her hand quickly and gave a quick nod to Jack. "See you inside." She spun on her heel, hesitating for the glass door to open—which seemed to take forever—and then rushed inside without hearing anything else. Blood rushed in her ears, and her heart nearly beat out of her chest.

But as she rolled the cart into the store, taking deep breaths and yanking the list from her purse, she paused by the glowing display of light fixtures.

All this time, Molly had never considered that she would be unrecognizable. She never looked in the mirror and said to herself, *Wow, you've changed.* But, more than that, not in a million years would she have thought she'd be forgotten. All Rochelle assumed was that she was a random relative helping Gran. Wouldn't she have considered that Molly Jansen, the granddaughter who lived in the farmhouse since she was eight, might be the first to come back?

Nope. She'd dished out so much to Molly over that last year of school. But obviously her memory failed. Or maybe, Chelle had just considered Molly a fly to be squished all those days. A big bully forgets their flies, don't they?

Molly pulled her shoulders back and headed to the light bulbs, feeling a little less tight and a little more like herself. No matter what, she was glad she'd got that out of the way. Facing the worst of her bullies. And the worst was a normal woman with a cute baby in tow. She'd grown up. Just like Molly had.

Maybe Polk Center had moved on, just like she had.

Jack shoved his hands in his pockets. Chelle gave him a quizzical look after Molly made a beeline into the store.

"That's Molly," he muttered. "You don't remember the Austins' granddaughter?"

Rochelle used both hands to tuck her loose strands behind her ears, her eyes rounded and her mouth fell open. "Oh my! I did not recognize her one bit. She was so…so awkward back then."

Jack shrugged his shoulders. "Not really. I don't remember her being that way." He remembered her being sad. A lot. "She's a big-time architect now."

"Wow. Wonder what happened to her mom." She lifted an eyebrow and shook her head. "She was a mess."

Yeah, and Rochelle didn't let Molly forget it, Jack recalled. "Well, Molly isn't a mess. She's doing well. I am helping her get Gertie's place ready to sell."

Rochelle brushed her hand over her daughter's crown and leaned back to look inside the store. "Well, tell her I'm sorry I didn't recognize her. Mom-brain." She laughed at her own joke and began to push her cart away.

Did she even remember how she had treated Molly?

Jack headed inside, worried that Molly was on the verge of tears like he remembered after her encounters with Rochelle James. He saw her waving at him from down the light-bulb aisle.

"Hey, do you know if Gran needs E-26 or E-12 bulbs

for the chandelier over the kitchen table?" Her ponytail whooshed as she scanned the top shelf on her tiptoes, then bent down to the second-from-the-bottom shelf.

"I am pretty sure these are what we need." He reached up and grabbed a box just above his head.

"Well, good thing I brought you along." Molly smirked. "I'd have never reached that without your help." Jack placed the box in her cart and chuckled.

They went through the rest of the list quickly. Molly was exceptionally attentive as he picked out a new router.

She looked at her watch. "If we can get home by eleven, I'll get that email sent in plenty of time."

"Email on a Sunday?"

"Ah, it's not about today. It's about sitting in my boss's in-box ready to open first thing on Monday." Molly began toward the front of the store. "But there is always a chance he's working anytime, any day. And in that case, he knows I am too." She winked.

"Seems like I have a thing to learn about corporate America. I breathe my work on Sundays by stepping outside for some fresh air. No need for plugs or screens."

"Are you considering entering corporate America, Jack?"

Jack shuffled up beside her as they passed the garden section. "Nah, I hope not." Molly eyed him with an arched brow. "No offense. But I'm banking on the next buyer to need a farming manager." He cleared his throat. "Did Gertie mention anything to you?"

"Oh, maybe. It's been a whirlwind." Molly blew a loose hair from her face.

"You think you can pass on that information to the real estate agent?" Jack clenched his teeth, feeling like the underdog asking the coach to put him in the game.

Molly stopped as they turned into the main aisle. She rested her elbow on the cart and studied him for a second. Of course Rochelle hadn't recognized her. The woman stood before him with a natural radiance unlike anything he remembered. No heavy eye makeup or hint of insecurity. Pretty lashes, blue eyes and glistening lips. Simply stunning. Just like yesterday. But instead of the somber shadow, she glowed with thoughtfulness. "I don't know about the real estate agent, Jack. I would hate for you to depend on that, though. You know…my friend created a dynamic website for job searches. She's gotten great reviews in *Forbes Magazine*, even. Would you like—"

A bitterness coated the back of his tongue. "No worries. I'm good." He clutched the cart and began to pull it toward self-checkout. Molly hesitated but then continued to check out the items as Jack handed them to her. He tried to shake away the unsettled feeling in the pit of his stomach.

As they were about to leave, Molly placed her hand on his arm. "Hey, I didn't mean to discard your desire to stay. We'll do what we can. I am certain Gran will demand it." She squeezed his forearm. "Just please…get that internet working." She widened her eyes and feigned a desperate plea slapping her hands together beneath her chin. She then giggled and said, "Not really kidding. I really do need you to fix that."

He chuckled. "You sure have changed, Molly Jansen." He reached out and tucked her hair behind her ear without even thinking. Her entire face froze, as did his finger just above her shoulder. "Oh, sorry. There's been a runaway hair all morning." He lifted his shoulders, then shoved his hand in his pocket. "Old habit, I guess."

Molly continued pushing the cart toward the parking lot. "Yeah, my hair is at this funky length…" She rolled her eyes and looked away, her cheeks flooding red.

His cell phone vibrated in his back pocket. Saved by the bell. Jack rolled his eyes at his own embarrassment and pulled his cell out. Lisa was calling. "Let me get this quick." If only she'd called a few seconds earlier. He'd have been saved from his awkwardness. "Hey, Lisa. What's up?"

"Hey, you aren't going to believe it."

"Wow, you sound hoarse."

"I think we are all sick. All at once." She coughed.

"Oh man. You think it's going around the baseball team?"

"Maybe, but you can't leave Tate here this week. I would feel horrible if he caught it."

"If he hasn't already."

"Jack!"

"I'll keep an eye on him. Don't worry. You all get better."

He ended the call just as Molly began to unload bags into the bed of his truck. He hesitated to approach, trying to calm the nerves that were a tangled mess in the pit of his stomach.

"Everything okay?" Molly asked over her shoulder.

"Nah, my sister's sick."

"Oh, I hope it's not too serious." She lifted two cans of paint and hefted them over the cart. Jack rushed up to help. They lowered the cans into the bed.

"Just a cold running through her family. But she watches Tate for me, so it's a double whammy."

"What do you mean?"

"I'm out of childcare for a couple days, at least. And,

worse, a simple cold could send Tate to the hospital."
He rubbed his cheek. "Just gotta watch him like a hawk
these next couple days." And figure out how to get some
work done in the meantime. Maybe he could ask Gertie
to help. She'd done it before.

This was exactly why he couldn't just pick up and
move to whatever job a headhunter would find for him.
Polk Center was the only place Tate had ever known,
and his family cared about Tate's well-being as much
as he did.

A day care would hardly warn him when a simple
cold was loose, and even if they did, what would a single dad do when his immunocompromised son needed
a plan B?

Chapter Eight

When they pulled up to the house, Molly wrestled with remorse for Jack's potential unemployment situation and her determination to get back to Chicago as fast as possible. Jack was obviously hoping for a favor—a way to keep his heels planted on this piece of Iowa indefinitely. Yet, Molly had only gotten this far by sticking her neck fully out in front, with not one distraction catching her unprepared. No time-consuming friendships or boyfriends. And certainly not a handsome single father who would lose sooner than later if Molly had her way with the timing of this farm sale. She grimaced knowing that it wasn't just about Jack. But he had a little boy to care for too.

They unloaded the truck and took everything into the kitchen. Jack got to work on the router, and Molly showed Gran the colors she'd picked for the kitchen and bathroom walls.

"It's so…gray." Gran scrunched her nose as she held up the swatch for the bathrooms.

"That's the trend these days." Molly dug in her purse and pulled out business cards. "I picked these up at the store's info center. A couple of contractors we can call to help with the bigger items…like replacing trim and fixing the loose boards on the porch. It will also give me some space to focus on real estate agents and such. Then we can at least get the ball rolling before I leave."

Gran released a long sigh. Shaking her head, she clutched her chin. "This is so overwhelming."

"Don't worry, Gran." Molly slid her arm around her shoulders. "I will make sure everything is set in place before I head out."

"When will that be?"

Molly wanted to say *as soon as possible*, but by the weariness in her grandmother's eyes and with the long list of things to accomplish, she thought it better of it. "Whenever you feel comfortable."

Gran exhaled again and said, "I guess Jack will fill in if needed."

Molly swallowed a huge lump of frustration and managed a smile. She couldn't shove away all her reservations about her high-school sweetheart and piece him into her fuzzy idea of family like Gran had.

Jack walked in from the living room. "I think it's ready. Want to give it a shot?"

"Wow, that was fast." Molly looked at her watch. "Just shy of eleven thirty." She rushed past him, trying to remain as nonchalant as possible. After their strange chemistry in the parking lot earlier, Molly diverted her thoughts to the biggest break of her life on her computer, keeping her mind at a good long distance from her heart. This house was enough to add to her plate. An old high-school boyfriend could not muddy up her vision for this visit. The guy still rubbed elbows with people like Rochelle. He was very much a shadow of a time forgotten.

Or, at least, shoved far to the back of her memory like those old Birkenstocks she wore in college—although, those had come back in fashion. Molly had certainly out-grown whatever inkling of similarity to life now was to life back then. Even Rochelle hadn't noticed her.

Molly exhaled and sat on her knees in the chair, pray-ing that the internet connection would work. She peered over her shoulder. An old Western played on the tele-vision while Tate was sound asleep on the couch. Must have crashed from all the sugar.

He was a cute kid. Had a personality too. Molly had hardly ever been around children. She'd never babysat as a teenager. Watching the internet symbol on her screen pulse as it tried to find a signal, Molly searched her mind for any moments of holding a baby.

Nope. One of her coworkers had been on maternity leave this past month, so maybe she'd have a chance. But really, she didn't understand the whole baby itch. The probability of that happening in her life was definitely a few years away. At least.

The *Connection Secured* prompt popped up. "Yes!" she squealed, then clasped her mouth, looking over her shoulder at the sleeping Tate. He stirred, fluttered his lashes, then settled back into his sugary sleep.

"It works, I take it?" Jack crossed over with a bright smile. Molly nodded.

Gran came up alongside him and handed Molly the business cards. "Here, dear. We don't need to call any-one. Jack and I worked it all out." She smiled up at him.

"You did?" Molly sat back in her chair, suddenly feel-ing like she was outnumbered—or, at least, she was being outplanned. She tossed the cards on the desk. "We need someone to help, Gran."

"Yes, we do. And Jack will be that someone. Just like his name: he's one of all trades." She giggled. "Jack needs me to watch Tate this week, and in exchange, he's willing to do all the work that you and I can't manage."

Molly stood, stuffing her hands in her back pockets. "Oh, I see."

"Daddy, you're back?" Tate called across the room, rubbing his eyes. Jack crossed over to him. "I'm thirsty." Jack gave him a piggyback ride to the kitchen.

Molly lowered her voice to Gran and said, "There's a reason we need a professional. If you want to sell fast, we need the work to be done well." Molly did not like the idea of spending every day with Jack. Besides the pictures of Mom on the wall, Jack was a living, breathing reminder of the road she'd tried to veer away from all these years.

"Of course." Gran wrung her hands and offered an assuring grin. "Jack is perfect for the job. And besides, I want family around during this time. Not some stranger walking in my last memories of this old place." She wistfully cast her eyes on the gallery spread of family pictures behind Molly. "You and Jack are it right now. And it's such a blessing to have you both fill in the gaps where Rob can't anymore." The corners of her mouth wobbled. She raised her brows at Molly. "Okay? Let's forget the contractors and just do this with the three of us."

Gran considered Jack family, and after hearing his kind words at Grandad's funeral, Molly shouldn't brush off Gran's attachment to Jack Behrens. While Molly was away, Jack had been welcomed with open arms in this space. She couldn't frame up any argument to resist Gran's suggestion. By the way her grandmother looked at her now, this wasn't just a suggestion but a mind made up.

"You're the boss, Gran. If that's what you want." Molly slid the cards from the desk and dropped them in the wastebasket. "If we can get everything heading in the right direction, then I'll plan on heading back at the end of next week. We have a lot of work ahead—" Molly's computer dinged. She spun around and opened her email. "Looks like I have this work to do now." Her boss wanted more than what she sent him. And it must be more pressing than she thought—it was Sunday, after all. She gave Gran her most assuring smile. "We'll get it all done, promise. I am just going to get to this real quick."

"Very good, dear." Gran patted her back. "I think I will take a quick nap."

Molly sat in her seat, shoving aside Austin Farm and focusing in on the work that required less emotion. Although, Molly's work excited her in a good way—a way that took all the precision and decision-making to a level of perfection. Nothing like an old house sagging at the seams and weeping with loss.

Jack worked on the simple projects around the house—changing bulbs, fixing Gran's toilet and organizing Rob's tools out in the garage with Tate—while Molly fell into her work at her computer.

After spending most of the afternoon in the garage, he walked into the room to gather up Tate's toys. Molly was engrossed at her screen, and maybe her nose was just a tad closer to it than before.

"You really needed that internet, didn't you?" Jack sat on the couch with a glass of iced tea, sliding toys into

Tate's backpack with his other hand. "Seems like you've been working on the longest email ever."

Molly sat back and cast a quick sideways glance over her shoulder. "Nope, it's become more than just a Sunday-afternoon email. This is the project of my life. Can't believe I might have a chance to see it go from the screen to an actual structure. It's just so cool to expand on it."

Jack chuckled. "Working on an old Iowa farmhouse is much less inspiring."

Molly pressed her shoulders back but didn't respond. She must have been caught up in her work. He gulped some tea and continued to clean up. The house was quiet. Tate and Gran had taken some stuff to the unlit burn pile at the back of the house. Zipping up Tate's backpack was the loudest noise in the place.

He scanned the wall with Molly's school portraits, landing on her high-school graduation photo, the girl he'd dated so long ago. Sitting in this living room with the grown-up version was surreal. She used to sit at that desk and draw, tossing her pencil aside as soon as he'd step into the room. Choosing him over her sketches. He hadn't thought about that in a long time. "I am not surprised that you're good at what you do. I remember your sketchbooks."

Molly swiveled in her seat. "You remember?"

He swirled his glass, adding to the quiet with clinking ice cubes. "Sure. You still have art hanging up in the high-school media center. I was there to speak at a 4-H meeting back in May."

She arched her eyebrows and smirked. "Huh. Never thought I would grace those halls—or walls—once I left."

"What made you choose architecture and not art?"

Molly cast her eyes on the back of the chair, tapping her finger and chewing on her lip. "Hmm, I guess it was practical. I was a general-studies major at first. Took an intro to design class." She breathed in deep and skimmed the room, noticeably avoiding the wall of pictures and peering up at the trim and the ceiling fan Jack had installed last summer. "Architecture is art." She fluttered her lashes and set her gaze directly at him. So much light and life in those blue eyes. As if she was part watercolor and part human. "But it also plays by a set of rules. You know, gravity for one." She laughed, but her lips hardly grew into a full-on smile. "I fell in love with the innovative projects and the control of a clean design, a pristine balsa-wood model, a…" she tapped her finger more forcefully, then her whole face brightened "…an untouched place. No breath, no words. Only space to be filled with better things." Maybe her eyes glistened with tears, not just life. But Jack knew that life was a mixture of breath and tears too. So Molly reflected life at its fullest right now. Life with heartache, memories and dreams.

A lump began to form in his throat. He dropped his gaze to the rim of his glass. "Sounds like you are doing exactly what you are supposed to be doing, Mol." He opened his mouth to apologize for using the nickname she had requested he not use, but when he looked up, she stood and walked over to the window beside the desk.

"I used to imagine the maze I'd build in the corn, and how I would steal away on Grandad's combine and make a secret room right in the center of the field."

Jack swallowed past the lump and released a hearty laugh. "Near impossible."

Molly pushed her shoulders up in a quick *I don't care*

movement and pressed down on a wooden slat to peer out the window. "It was a comforting thought for me. And when I got to that design class in college, my memory of that secret room spurred me on." She inhaled loudly and spun around, shoving her hands in her pockets. "The rest is history."

Jack stood now. "I didn't expect such a heartfelt answer." He tapped his boot gently against the coffee table leg.

"And you?" Molly reached over and grabbed her empty coffee mug. "I recall you thought about trying to redshirt for the ISU football team back when we knew each other." Her face had lost all emotion. She asked about him as if he was a complete stranger. Or in a way like she didn't really care about his story. She continued. "I mean, besides all your plans about your next game and the next party at Derrick What's-his-name's." He half expected her eyes to roll around at the snark coating her words. Jack grimaced inwardly. Why would she act excited to hear his story now? He'd broken her heart back then.

He crossed over and leaned on the other side of the window, peering out at the back of the garage building where the old '42 tractor sat in its eternal grave amid some wooden planters of trailing petunias. Molly stepped back and crossed her arms with the mug hooked on her finger.

"I wouldn't blame you for not caring one lick about my story, Molly." Her mouth opened as if she would protest, but he just shook his head and mouthed *No worries.* He sighed, leaning his head on the window trim. "I did what most country boys around here do. Agriculture and settling down." He resisted the pity party that swelled in his chest. Settling down to be uprooted at the highest bidder of this place. No, he would not keep begging for help. That's not the kind of person he'd ever wanted to be. Molly and Gertie knew his situation. And he needed to trust they would try to put in a good word in for him with the next owner.

He sucked in a staggered breath. Trust was hard for Jack. A shield the size of this house stood between his heart and trust. All the pain of watching his wife slip away amid the advice to just trust—the doctors, the treatments, God—had seemed to be lip service at the time, leaving him a widower with a hole in his heart from all the empty promises that trust was supposed to bring. Molly stood in the shadow of his own empty promise to her—to be there when her mom left for good—not just as a high-school boyfriend but as a friend.

She'd gotten past it, that was for sure. And he would have to do what his father told him when he had decided to sell the restaurant. "Next steps, son. That's all we've got."

Molly squinted and half smiled as she seemed to watch Gran and Tate outside. He couldn't see them from his angle, but he could sure see Molly. Skipping away from the messy puddle in his heart, Jack said, "I am so glad you've found your purpose. Purpose is a beautiful thing." He winked, the word *beautiful* echoing in his mind, tripping up his heart to consider the beauty standing before him. Those watercolor eyes sparkled. "One day, I might come to Chicago and see a Molly Jansen original."

Molly's eyes rounded. She tucked her chin down and backed to the kitchen. "That might be a long time coming, Jack Behrens." She winked back, then turned on her heel and said over her shoulder, "Maybe you'll own this place by then?" She chuckled.

He laughed also. "Man, that would be something." He knocked on the wall with his fist. That would be something, indeed.

Chapter Nine

The next morning, Molly woke up just past six to a loud humming sound. The fast beat of machinery sounded like a small tractor sat beneath her bedroom. "What in the world?" She flung her legs around, put on her slippers, grabbed her robe and headed downstairs. She could almost feel the rumble travel up from the floorboards to the heels of her feet.

She peered past the wall and over the banister halfway down the staircase. Jack and Gran stood on either side of Grandad's recliner where Tate sat. He wore some sort of life jacket hooked up with black hoses to a machine on the floor beside the chair.

"H-h-h-i-i-i M-m-m-i-ss M-o-o-lly!" Tate waved his hand, his whole body vibrating.

"Did we wake you up, dear?" Gran took a few steps toward her. "We're getting all set up with Tate's treatments."

Molly swiped at her eyes and raked her fingers through her hair, suddenly aware that she had literally just rolled out of bed. She continued down the rest of the stairs, cast a quick glance at the small mirror by the front door. Good. At least she looked…decent.

Molly stood next to Gran, tying her robe over her pajamas. "What is that?"

Jack adjusted a clear plastic mask over Tate's mouth, carefully placing its elastic band around the little boy's head. He turned on another smaller machine chugging nearly as loud as the monster vest. "This is a breathing treatment with some meds to help clear his lungs." Jack squatted beside Tate and winked at him, then cocked his head toward the women. "And this—" he yanked at the vest "—is his super vest. Gets him all ready for hero stuff." This time, he winked at Molly, then turned to Tate who gave him two thumbs-up.

Jack jumped up and asked, "Mind if we turn the TV on? Helps him pass the time."

"Sure." Gran handed him the remote. Jack found a show and cranked up the volume. The house was as loud as a Chicago rush hour. Molly slipped into the slightly quieter kitchen and poured the last of the coffee while Gran pulled out a tub of cream cheese from the fridge and some bagels from the breadbox.

Jack crossed over to the back door and fiddled with his keys. "You sure you don't mind all this, Gertie?"

"Of course not. We'll take good care of him." Gran patted his shoulder as she took her armful to the table. "He wears that for thirty minutes?"

"Yes, he has a timer on his watch. Pretty good about it."

Molly leaned against the far counter with her cup, beginning to feel self-conscious in her bed attire. "So hero stuff, huh?"

Jack chuckled. "Well, CF-style. That's the vest that breaks up the mucus in his lungs."

"He does that every day?"

"Yep, twice a day since he was a baby." Jack sipped from his travel mug. "He's always been a trooper. He loves to hear his voice wobble with that thing—even before he could talk." His dimples appeared in full force. He grinned so wide his eyes crinkled. "And he always plays along with the superhero stuff." He shook his head as if mesmerized by a thought. He cast a gaze to the living-room door and said, "He's better than a superhero. The kid is amazing."

Molly shifted in her slippers and stared down at the caramel tint of her coffee with cream. She recalled what Jack had said yesterday about purpose, that it was a beautiful thing. More beautiful from this beaming father than any high-end residence or well-planted cornfield. She forced herself to look up again. Dismantling her guard against an old boyfriend, she studied Jack with fresh eyes. The father of a superhero stood tall and handsome. His honey-brown hair slid across his forehead as he, too, focused on his mug. He sipped it again and breathed in so deep his broad chest expanded beneath his John Deere T-shirt. His eyes shone right at her. Looking away was not an option. He trapped her with that beautiful purpose he'd mentioned. Amber flecks glowing with life—no doubt, love of a man who cared so deeply for the little boy who amazed him.

But what blunted Molly's willpower to look away was that ever-present softness she'd hardly remembered from knowing Jack a decade ago. Unlike the platonic, cool exchanges of colleagues and acquaintances back in Chicago, Molly fell into Jack's gaze as if it was the one place in all of Iowa that offered what she desperately needed and hadn't realized until now. His familiar affection captured her in a comfort she'd lost over the years of hard work and nose to the drawing board— quite literally. Jack Behrens had lived so much life as far as she could tell, but even so, he magnified something Molly hadn't longed for in forever, but now her whole spirit ached for it.

Home.

Not this old farmhouse or even Gran's company.

She wanted so desperately to be home—not in a place—but with a person.

"Well, I better head out. Have a couple meetings today." Jack's words didn't quite match up to his lips. Molly was so focused on his face her ears didn't register his words. She looked down at her coffee again, a refuge for her embarrassment, sipped it and walked to the table. "See you all later."

"Bye, Jack. Don't worry about Tate," Gran called as she smeared some cream cheese on a bagel. The door creaked open, then shut softly. "Molly, you seem off in your own world. Everything okay?"

"Oh yeah, it's fine." Molly mustered up a nonchalant smile. Gran hooked an eyebrow. "He's a good dad, huh?"

Gran nodded and sighed. "One of the best. Hopefully we can help him continue on at this place."

"I'm afraid that's going to be a tricky thing, finding a buyer and an employer for a built-in farm manager." Molly clicked her tongue. For the first time, though, she took Jack's request seriously. "I am not sure what kind of real estate agent to hire for that."

"Well, there's a new one in town. He might be helpful, being in this area and all."

"In Polk Center?"

Gran said, "Mmm-hmm" and slid a bagel to Molly.

"Ugh," Molly blurted and sat down. Gran lifted her brow in surprise. "Sorry, just wasn't expecting to head into town here, not with Des Moines so close by. Bigger, more strangers. You know?"

"Molly Jansen, you've grown up. Look at you. Nobody is going to say one word about anything. High school is over."

"True. Saw a classmate yesterday, actually. She didn't even remember me."

Gran tilted her head and began on the next bagel. "That's not a compliment, I guess. Not being remembered."

"It was a relief. You don't want to know the things they used to say to me about Mom—"

Gran held up her hand to stop her, a dab of cream cheese on her fingertip.

Molly gathered in a breath. "Anyway, if you think the real estate agent could help, then we can try. I'm all grown-up, right?"

"You are. And you should be proud of yourself too. Personally, I'd like to show you off to all those gossip-mongers."

Molly rolled her eyes. "I really don't need any praises. Wish Mom's story was different, though." She grimaced and picked at her breakfast.

"Me too, dear." Gran pressed the lid on the cream cheese and twisted the plastic tie around the bagel bag. "Remember, it's her story, not yours." She leaned over and kissed Molly's head. "Exactly why you should walk into Polk Center with your head high. You're brilliant."

"Brilliant?" Molly chuckled and shook her head. "Not yet. Hoping to get there soon, though."

"Oh darling, you are too humble. We are thrilled for you in this very moment." Gran's hand flung to her mouth. "Look at me, speaking for Grandad as if—" Her eyes filled, and the corners of her mouth twitched into a fragile smile. She whispered, "We really are, though. I believe he still thinks that too."

The chugging of the machine on the other side of the wall filled the silence between them. "You are too kind, Gran. I think Jack said it best—" Molly swallowed past a lump forming in her throat "—that little guy is truly the amazing one." It felt good to deflect the attention to a four-year-old, especially when her heart lurched at the mention of Grandad—another amazing guy who'd been pretty super around here.

When Jack walked into Gertie's kitchen just past three o'clock, he wondered if he was in the right house. Instead of the yellow wallpaper warming the room like a soft buttery biscuit, the bare plaster shone bright white, like the meringue of a chocolate pie. The color of the cabinets was a near match to a pie's toasty peaks.

Molly stood on a step stool in front of the pantry door at the back of the kitchen, cleaning the wall just above the door frame.

"Wow, this is quite a change." Jack shoved his hands in his pockets and crossed to her.

"Will have to wait for the walls to dry before I paint." Molly continued to scrub. Bits of wallpaper clung to her old Polk High T-shirt, and all along the frayed edge of her cutoffs.

"Looks like pretty messy business." He picked a piece off her shirt sleeve and laughed.

"Hey, hard work is hardly neat." Her ponytail wagged back and forth as she spoke. "Spent most of the time taking off that wallpaper." She nodded to a massive pile of wallpaper scraps pushed up against the wood wainscoting by the table. "Don't think I will be able to feel my biceps for a few days." Molly took her sponge from the wall, plopped it in the bucket on the counter, then stepped down, stretching her neck back and forth.

"I could've helped." He reached over and squeezed her shoulder without thinking. Only wanting to comfort. Her eyes grew wide, just like his, and he dropped his hand. "Okay, weird personal-space moment." He laughed and rubbed the back of his neck.

Molly shifted her weight and wiped her hands on her shorts. They both looked around the kitchen. He wasn't sure if Molly was pretending to inspect her work, but he sure was. All he could really think about was how easy it had been for him to want to care for her, to want to help, to want to be here by her side more than any other place he'd ventured today—the John Deere dealer, the seed company, the back quarter of land to chat with the detasseling crew. All those places seemed like stepping-stones to get to this destination, right here, right now, with cute Molly Jansen. She took her phone from her pocket, glanced at it, then looked up again. Her ponytail stirred up a flowery scent, her cheeks pinked beneath dazzling blue eyes, and her button chin, crumpling into tens of dimples as she worked hard to pay attention to her work. Or at least, he assumed she was pretending to.

Especially when she straightened her shoulders and tilted her head. "Hey." Her voice was sweet, a pitch higher than normal. Whoa! The flashback of her cute banter as a teen jump-started his heart into a tiny stampede. Molly the architect became Molly the pretty girl in bio class who would wait at his locker between classes. "Do me a favor?"

She'd said the same thing back then, hadn't she? If he recalled correctly, she'd needed to borrow his notes after missing class the day before.

"Always," he said now, just like he said then, completely stuck in this strange time warp that revved up his pulse.

Did she remember too? Her teeth rested on her bottom lip and her blues boomeranged back and forth, searching his face. Jack ignored the resistance of his practical self and took a step forward, inching his hands from his pockets.

Molly scrunched her nose and opened her mouth to speak but didn't say a word, only took in a short breath and cleared her throat. Her shoulders slumped as she stared up at him with a less-than-familiar stony disposition. "Take the paper out to the trash? I've got to return a text." She passed by him quickly and headed to the living room.

Hmm, maybe Jack was reading into things.

Molly continued typing on her phone while sliding a cool gaze to him and nodded toward the paper. His heart thumped with embarrassment and maybe something else.

He gathered up the scraps of paper and headed out the back door, carefully down the steps and to the trash can beside the garage.

"Daddy!" Tate ran up the gravel driveway, leaving Gertie beside her garden fence. She waved above her

large, brimmed sun hat. "Look what I got." Tate held out
a basket filled with mulberries. The dark purple juice
stained the corners of his mouth. "Gran took me on a
walk by the creek. There are a gazillion berries there."

"Yum." Jack grabbed a couple and popped them in
his mouth. "Tastes like summer." Gertie came up behind Tate. "Hope it went okay today."

"Of course." Gertie tousled Tate's hair. "We inspected
outside the whole house, didn't we, Tate?"

"Yes, and you've got some work to do, Dad." Tate
pushed his eyebrows up nearly to his dark brown hair-
line. "We might have to sleep here."

Jack laughed. "We've got daylight till nearly ten
o'clock. I am sure we can get plenty done and get you
tucked into your own bed." They followed Gertie to the
front porch at her request.

"I am worried about the porch, Jack. Looks like
there's rot." She ascended the porch steps and pointed
to the post to the right of the steps. "Think you can replace it? I don't want this house to seem like it's hanging on by a thread to any potential buyers." She stared
off across to the main road and the soybean fields in the
distance. "Rob would have had none of that."

"Of course, Gertie. Don't you worry." Jack knelt and
pushed on the wood. It crumbled beneath his finger. He
clenched his teeth and began to think how he might do
this. "I will probably need an extra pair of hands."

"I can help!" Tate wrapped his arms around the post.

"Nah, bud. Someone a little taller."

"How 'bout me?" Molly spoke through the screen of
the open front door.

"You sure your biceps can handle it?" Jack teased,

smirking as he crossed his arms and pulled his baseball cap down, then up.

Molly pushed through the door. "Won't bother me one bit." She offered a bright, unassuming grin. "I can't feel my biceps, remember?" They both laughed. Jack rubbed his jaw and shook his head, reluctantly looking back at the post.

Tate huffed. "I am strong too."

"Yes, you are, superhero." Gertie squeezed his shoulder. "I think I need you in the kitchen, though. Can you handle an electric mixer?"

Tate's mouth fell, and his eyes grew big. "I sure can." He jumped up and pushed past Molly, running through the screen door. It slammed against the frame.

"Hey, bud, be careful," Jack called.

Molly followed the four-year-old and said over her shoulder, "Just going to make sure I saved everything on my computer. I'll be back in a second."

Laughter and Gertie's singsong voice floated from the house as Jack headed to the garage to get some supplies. Yep, this was a fine place to land after a day of working. And not just because of the property he'd grown to love. But the company too.

He caught a glimpse of Molly's black Honda Civic parked in front of the garage. She had sped into that driveway, sparking his memory, and chasing away the gloom he'd never quite shaken this past year. Sure, she was an inspiration. Living her dream after surviving her own nightmares. But what was this effect Molly had on him? A renewed appreciation for an old girlfriend, or forgotten feelings relighting a flame after a lifetime of being extinguished?

He shook his head and peered out at her car again,

catching sight of the Illinois license plates. Jack sighed and turned all his focus on the task at hand. That was all a farmer could do when he was working against the clock.

Chapter Ten

Molly wished she could have come up with a better way to react to Jack's thoughtfulness in the kitchen. If she was honest with herself, a million tiny butterflies swarmed her stomach at his gentle squeeze, and she should have assured Jack he had done nothing wrong. Ten years ago, his consideration would have been exactly right. He was sweet back then. Playful and flirtatious in the school hallways and on their dates. But caring about her in such a genuine way? In the months after they broke up, she'd convinced herself that he didn't have it in him.

Jack Behrens was there for her now—for her and Gran. And Molly couldn't keep her mind consumed with the important stuff—like that work text she received. She should have been thankful to be saved by the bell... or her phone. But after sorting out the needs from the office and watching Jack gather up the wallpaper scraps and trudge out the back door, she could only focus on the repercussion of their awkward encounter in the kitchen, and how much she wished she had taken that hand on her shoulder and...

Okay, enough.

After she finished up on her computer, Molly waited a few minutes for Jack to return from the garage, pushing herself on the old porch swing and keeping an eye across the driveway.

"He might need your help gathering things in the garage." Gran called from the far side of the living room. Molly could just see her figure through the screen door.

"All right," Molly replied and pushed off the swing, steadied it, then jogged down the steps and along the flagstone path to the side of the garage.

She stood in the doorway of Grandad's favorite place besides the cab of a combine. It smelled like sawdust, metal and wood glue. Bracing herself with a hand on either side of the door, she closed her eyes and savored the memory of the tall, lean man slightly hunched over the workbench. His precision with his work was what Molly remembered most. Even when he would take out a knife to simply sharpen a pencil—the old-fashioned way, she would say—his long careful strokes were never rushed. His attention was fully dedicated to his task, and the cadence of his quiet words would match the methodical action of his hand.

"See there, Molly-Moo. We never had those fancy electric sharpeners in my day," he had muttered. "I don't think they are a match to my pocketknife, anyway."

And Molly would lean her cheek on her fist and gather the curled shavings one by one. Grandad always seemed to be with her when she'd used that pencil for her homework. And even though she had a sharpener of her own, she would find Grandad whenever she needed it sharpened again. He was right. There was nothing like a pencil sharpened by hand—especially his.

How had she forgotten his special technique all these years? Did she once recall his method when she sat in an architecture studio in the wee hours of the mornings? No. But she could guarantee that Grandad thought of her all the time. Every visit, he would say something about Iowa missing out on the little spitfire, Molly-Moo, all grown-up.

But was he actually saying that he missed Molly-Moo, the grown-up?

Molly's eyes fluttered open. The spot where Grandad would stand had a couple four-by-four posts leaning against the workbench. Jack walked toward her with a drill case in one hand and a wood block in the other. "Hey there, are you okay?"

Molly inhaled deeply. She stepped into the dim place and met Jack at the corner of the bench.

She brushed her hand along its surface. "Just remembering."

Jack set the drill case down and leaned an elbow on it. "Yeah, it's got Rob all over it. Always sense him close when I come in here."

Molly's chest constricted. Every tool was hung just right on the pegboard. The workbench had not one bit of clutter, save the case Jack had placed on it. The garage was in order like Molly remembered it. Like Grandad had left it.

"Guess my grandfather passed down his love of order to me." Molly laughed softly. "He was nothing like… Mom." She grimaced at mentioning her to Jack.

Jack's elbow dropped from the case, and he slid his hand along the table just across from her own. "You are definitely Rob's granddaughter. Just seeing your hard work on that computer."

Molly's eyes throbbed with emotion. She couldn't speak. These past twenty-four hours were so consumed with getting this place ready, she'd forgotten the integral component to Austin Farm—the man who'd poured his heart and soul into it for nearly five decades.

Jack turned his back to the bench and fiddled with the wooden block. It was about a foot long and probably a third in thickness. He spun it around and around like the blades of a combine. "I spent many hours working out here with Rob. And out in the fields. I miss those conversations during harvest." His dimple appeared, but his voice held little amusement.

"Did he make you drink hot tang tea?" Molly placed both elbows on the work surface.

Jack looked over at her. "Yeah, he did. Wasn't bad. The spice and sweetness will forever mark late nights in a John Deere cab."

Molly nodded. "Sounds like you probably took my place when I left."

Jack shifted, and he seemed to open his mouth to speak.

"No, don't worry," Molly answered, straightening. "I am glad you were there with him. You seem like a great friend, Jack. To my grandparents." And to Molly, if she was honest. The past couple conversations with him had only been cut off because of Molly's resistance to growing soft. "I really don't know how to be. I wasn't ready for this."

Jack turned to face her again, placing the block beside the drill case. "Nobody was." This time, she allowed him to rub her shoulder without flinching. She couldn't look directly into his eyes, but she gave an assuring smile, patted his arm, then stepped back on a deep intake of air. Jack was talking about Grandad's death, and he was one hundred percent right in the unpreparedness for such a tragedy. But if Molly was one hundred percent truthful to herself, she meant she wasn't ready for him. For Jack Behrens to be more than a blast from the past, but rather a grown man whose own hard knocks had softened all his edges.

Molly offered to help Jack take all the supplies to the porch. He followed her out with the large posts, while she carried the drill case and two blocks.

"So you really know how to fix that post?" Molly called over her shoulder as she carefully crossed the flagstones. "Did Grandad pass on his woodworking knowledge to you, or is that something they teach in ag these days?"

Her snarky tone had him answer with a laugh. He squinted as they turned toward the porch. The sun was as bright as it should be in an Iowa July.

Molly set the stuff on the porch, then climbed up the steps. She turned around, offering her hands out. Jack carefully handed her the pieces, and they laid them down on the other side of the front door. "Seriously. How do you know what to do?"

He pulled out his phone from his back pocket, leaned it against the windowsill and answered, "YouTube." Molly laughed, and the whole day brightened. Her face was glowing after the gloom just moments before. And the fact that he had caused her a small piece of joy? Well, it made him smile too.

"I actually had to do something similar for my dad when he sold his duplex. I pretty much know most of the steps, but YouTube is handy for tips."

"It sure is." Molly stuck her hands in the back pockets of her cutoffs. She tilted her head and looked at him with one eye shut, blocking out the sun. "How do you think I got that wallpaper off in record time?" Copper highlights around her oval face shone in the sunshine, and each little freckle was obvious on her button nose.

"Great minds…" Jack pointed to his head then to hers "…watch YouTube."

Molly saluted. "Absolutely." Full-on playfulness. It suited her well.

Jack lifted his baseball cap and ran his hand through his hair. "All right, we need to brace the overhang with some faux posts. Then I can remove the rotten one and see how much decay there is. Hopefully it's just a small part that we can replace."

They worked on putting the posts in place.

"Funny, when I was younger, this place seemed like the one steady place on all the earth." Molly held onto the old post as Jack worked on detaching it from the overhang. "My safe haven. Guess it held up during the seasons I needed it most."

Jack paused and glanced down at her. "This place gave you a great jumping-off point, Molly. You grew those wings and flew." He continued to work. Molly didn't say anything. But Jack's mind was reeling like an old videotape on rewind, screeching and jumping through the long hospital stays with little Tate sitting on the bed beside his mama, those hard nights after Brittany's death, the late-night dinners with Rob and Gertie with kindness like a warm blanket for his shivering insides. And the hard, consuming work of growing crops to keep busy, steady. This place held up in the seasons he had needed it most too.

Thing was, he couldn't imagine himself letting go just yet. The post suddenly released from the trim, and he and Molly held it together. The house was not doing one thing to keep it upright anymore.

Molly laid her end of the post carefully across the table saw. Jack took his pocketknife and poked around the end. "Yep, totally rotten up to...here." He rested the blade along the edge of the post. "Think you could mark it?"

Molly grabbed one of Grandad's pencils from the open toolbox and marked the post. "There you go."

"Perfect." He closed his knife and traded it for the plastic protective glasses in his front pocket. As he slid them on, he warned her. "You should probably step back unless you've got glasses too. Don't want anything happening to your—" Jack pressed his lips together and his Adam's apple bobbed against his collar. "Your eyes, I mean."

Molly gave a thumbs-up and jogged over to the steps, several feet away, all the while wondering if he had coined a term for her eyes. She sat and wrapped her arms around her knees, trying to calm a giddy curiosity. *Your baby blues?* Eh, nothing to get head over heels about. How about *beautiful blues*? Molly rolled her eyes at her ridiculous pondering. But just the thought of Jack speaking something endearing to her jump-started old high-school feelings.

The saw ground her thoughts to a happy end, and she forced herself to check her email on her phone while she waited. Nothing important. But a text popped up from her assistant.

Caught a glimpse at Harleson's design. Not too shabby.

Molly gritted her teeth. She stood and shoved her phone in her pocket, promising to leave it alone until she could sit at her computer. The saw quieted. "Ready to get this finished?" Her voice cracked.

"Getting there."

Gran pushed the screen door open. For a brief second, Molly thought how it might be better if Gran helped Jack, and Molly babysat Tate inside—if babysitting meant setting the boy in front of the TV and Molly working at her computer.

Tate appeared with a platter. "Look what we made!"

Molly took the porch steps two at a time and picked up a chocolate chip cookie. "Nice. And that plate... That was my favorite." Farm animals peeked out from under the cookies. She squatted down so she was eye level with Tate. "Have you ever gone to the farm area at the zoo?" she asked Tate softly.

He scrunched his nose and said, "Yeah, but I like the lions best. You can't pet those." Tate's eyes grew wide and then he grimaced into a growl.

"Wow, you are really good at that." She feigned surprise. "Superhero and lion?" Molly glanced over at Jack.

He chuckled and said, "Always keeps me on my toes."

Molly turned back to Tate. "I think Gran might have some matching cups if you want some lemonade too."

The plate wobbled in Tate's hands. "Can I pour the jug? I am really good at that too."

Molly gently took the plate and set it on the porch swing. "I could use some help, sure." She bit her cookie and widened her eyes. "Yum, Tate. These are delicious."

"He did most of the work," Gran said dotingly.

"Oh yeah." Tate ran back to the plate and grabbed a cookie for himself.

"I'll get your beads, Tater," Gran said, pushing through the back door. "I can pour the lemonade too."

"No, I can do it." He pushed past her, then spun around and stared up at Molly. "Come on, Miss Molly. Show me those cups." The little boy's face was so lit up with eagerness, Molly would have expected he misunderstood she meant cups and not the actual animals themselves.

Molly giggled. She wiped the corner of her mouth and boomeranged a look from Gran to Jack. "Oh, I am sure Gran knows better—"

"I am sure he's ready for a fresh face. We've been together all morning. Go on, dear." Gran grinned. "You'll need to help him with the medicine bottle cap. The cups are in their usual place."

Molly followed Tate inside. The little guy ran into the kitchen, flung open the fridge door and began to grab the lemonade jug from the shelf.

"Whoa there," Molly exclaimed, helping him just before the sloshing lemonade splashed all over the eggs.

"I am a really good helper," Tate tooted, rubbing his hands together.

"I see that." Molly set the jug on the counter. "You need your…um…beads?"

"Oh yeah!" He lifted his arm in the air like a superhero taking off, then zipped across the kitchen to the table and grabbed a medicine bottle nearly as big as his head. "Can you get the lid?"

"Yes, sir." Molly undid the lid and took out the giant pills. "Yikes, Tate! These are massive."

"Super massive." He broke apart the pill and poured

tiny beads into his mouth like he had done before eating a doughnut yesterday. "See? Easy." His sweet grin prodded his freckled cheeks just beneath his long lashes.

She couldn't help but tap his nose. "You impress me."

"I do?" His head cocked to one side. "But I haven't shown you my super-cool moves, yet."

Molly laughed. "But you take medicine like it's nothing. I would never have done that at your age."

"You wouldn't have?"

"No way. I would run under the table and clamp my mouth shut until Gran had to drag me out by the ankles." Tate's eyes grew so wide, and his grin flipped upside down so quickly, Molly realized she was taken very literally. "Oh, not really by the ankles." Tate's shoulders dropped in relief. "But I just did not like the taste at all."

"It takes lots of special powers, Miss Molly." Tate pushed his chest out. "I've been growing those powers since I was this big." He held his fingers apart with a space just as big as one of those giant pills.

Molly couldn't help but laugh again. "Wow, that's a long time, Tate."

"Sure is." He dragged a chair to the counter. "Now back to the lemonade."

When they had poured cups for everyone, Molly waited for Tate to use the restroom. He didn't want her to go outside without him, so she held the tray of cups and stood beside the door. It didn't seem there was any work going on outside, just a conversation between Gran and Jack. She tried not to listen, but when she heard her name, Molly just couldn't help but strain her ear to the screen door.

"Yeah, she's tenacious. Her future seems bright, Gertie."

"I know. Just a shame she couldn't have spent more time with Rob. He was so proud of her. Missed her fiercely when she first left." Gran sighed. "You wouldn't have known him that way, Jack."

"Yeah, I was the enemy back then."

"You know Rob had to side with his granddaughter and not the football star who broke her heart."

"I know. But when I won you all over again, Rob still talked about Molly all the time. I don't know that I believed how great she was—is—until I saw for myself."

"Ah, what's that, Mr. Behrens? I haven't seen that twinkle in your eye since… Well, I don't know that you've seemed so…happy, in quite a long time."

"Happy?" Jack guffawed. "I am just…impressed. Gotta find some steady ground before I can claim any kind of happy."

"Jack, we will do our best to get you hired on—"

"I know you will. But thinking I need to also figure out how to spread my own wings, with or without this."

Tate barreled into the living room. "Ready!" He rushed to the door and slammed it open with both hands. "C'mon, Miss Molly." And she took a deep breath in, pushed all she had just heard to the back of her mind and walked out of the house, confident and steady like the sidekick of a mighty superhero.

Chapter Eleven

The rest of the day, Jack and Molly worked on the porch with bellies full of lemonade and chocolate chip cookies. When they finished, they ran down the steps and stood side by side beneath a golden sky. Tate rode by on the old John Deere pedal tractor and cried, "Yippee!"

Jack admired the pure admiration on Molly's face as she cheered for Tate, then locked her gaze with his. Her laugh lines were a fine tribute to the joy glistening in her beautiful blues.

"Cute kid, Jack," she murmured and knocked him with her shoulder as she turned to face their work. With a quick upward glance through her lashes, she said, "He's got that same ability to win over girls like someone I knew in high school." She added in a whisper, "Better teach him to be a gentleman."

"Hey," Jack protested. "I wasn't anything but…"

She turned her face toward him, one eye closed to a pesky ray of sunshine, and with a broad, unassuming smile. "Don't worry. You're good."

He tried to mirror such an easy grin, but his pulse pounded wildly. This moment seemed to be so much more than playful banter. He could only manage a slight smile, taking in every speck of gold in her blue eyes and sprinkle of freckles on her ivory skin as if he was memorizing the girl who might not come around for another decade—or ever.

Her whole demeanor changed, and she shifted on her feet. Black strands of hair fell across her brow, and her ponytail swung as she studied their work. "Looks as good as new."

Jack followed her gaze. "Yep, we make a good team, Mol—ly." He nudged her. "Old habits are hard to break."

"No worries." She brushed her fingers along her brow, pushing her hair behind her ear. "Hard to do when we are in such a place as this. Chock-full of memories…" Did she slide her attention to their—or rather, the Austins'—porch swing? "But always a safe haven for the down-and-out."

"Ain't that the truth?" Jack whistled and ran his hand through his hair.

Jack finished cleaning up the tools and old wood while Tate insisted Molly race him down the drive. If Tate was anything like this with his Aunt Lisa, Jack owed her more than a thank-you every day.

"He's going to wear you out," Jack called to Molly who was hunched over trying to catch her breath.

"Eh, better workout than my building's gym back in Chicago." She flexed her arm like a bodybuilder. Jack shook his head on a chuckle.

But while Molly caught her breath, her attention snagged on her watch. She stood and stretched her arms behind her. "Hey, Tater, I have to go work on some stuff. How 'bout we race some more tomorrow?"

Tate's shoulders fell, but Jack was able to give him a warning look with a hooked eyebrow.

Tate moped and said, "Okey dokey."

Molly patted his head, then jogged past Jack. "Good kid, there," she affirmed again. "We're going to head to evening service at church."

Jack tried to keep his eyes on the tools he collected in his arms, but he couldn't help looking back at Molly as she disappeared inside. He was certain that Gertie saying Rob missed her fiercely was an understatement.

If he could see her now...

Gerite appeared at the door. "Thanks, Jack. You all want to come in and have some dinner?"

"Nah, we'll grab something on the way. It's getting late. Got to get home."

Tate climbed into the truck, and they headed out.

While Tate watched TV during his evening treatment, Jack sat down at the old desktop in the spare bedroom. He glanced around the room and down the hall lined with frames of photos arranged perfectly by Brittany's eye for decor. Sitting at the desk, he ran his finger along the keyboard, thinking about all the papers Brittany had written on this thing. She had been well on her way to a master's degree in education.

From the other room, Tate coughed as the vest shook his little body, loosening all the gunk that lowered his lung function. The reason Brittany had wanted to be an educator was to have the same school schedule as Tate, and to become a strong advocate for his health needs by understanding the internal workings of the school district. Her passing away left both Jack and Tate floating in uncertainty about what lay ahead. His sister and the Austins offered a sense of security for Jack while he cared for Tate alone.

Jack opened his email and scrolled through his contacts. He had a few connections in different parts of the state. But, just as Molly had hunkered down at Austin Farm for those hard seasons, Jack had done the same. High-school graduation was the big showstopper for Molly to take her bow and fly away. Now it seemed an obvious end to Jack's sheltering at the Austin place came with Gertie placing the farm on the market. He had known this all along, but just couldn't separate fear from reason.

Jack hovered the mouse over the contact of a consultant he knew from Northwest Iowa. He shoved his back into the chair. Molly had been brave and moved away to start a new life. Maybe it was time for Jack to do the same. Be brave. Find a way to work and provide for Tate, even if that meant a stranger caring for his needs during the day. Even if that meant Jack working for a paycheck and not farming land. Even if it meant having a boss and colleagues, not a family to farm with.

Was he brave enough? The thing was, Molly was brave for herself. Jack had to be brave for himself *and* his son. So far, he hardly felt adequate with keeping up with Tate's needs on a daily basis. The few people in his life he could trust were his only saving grace.

Besides, picking up and trying something new would not only have him turn away from Austin Farm, but he would have to walk away from this house, the one place where Brittany seemed close, and he would have to leave Polk Center, the only home he'd ever known.

Molly was thankful to go to church with Gran that evening. She'd enjoyed the songs and the preaching, realizing how much she missed that part of growing up in Polk Center. Church was a treat when she was little because it meant she was spending time with her grandparents. And then when Mom left, church had been a constant—until the church walls weren't strong enough to shield her from whispers, stares and loaded questions at the coffee hour.

After a late dinner, Molly set to work while Gran sorted out old bins in her master closet. Molly powered down her computer about an hour after Gran said goodnight. She walked over to the couch and pulled off the quilt, wrapping it around her shoulders and settling in the recliner to jot down some notes before heading up to bed.

A thud sounded out on the porch. Molly jumped up. An image of the newly attached porch post crashing down invaded her mind, and she ran around the couch to the front door. Pulling down the blinds, she peeked out the sidelight window. Jack stepped into the warm glow of the porch light.

Molly opened the door, stuck her head out and whispered, "What are you doing here—"

"Hi, Miss Molly." Tate was in his pajamas leaning against the porch swing. "I forgot my toy." He scrambled beneath the swing and fished it out. "See?" The little boy held up a six-inch plush action figure.

Molly stepped outside and took care to close the screen door without a noise. She bundled the blanket into a ball at her torso. The heat of the day had yet to dissipate completely.

Jack guided Tate away from the swing with a soft hand on his back and said, "Sorry to startle you, Molly. He can't sleep without it." Tate yawned and rubbed his eyes. "Tried to be quiet, but that's tricky for us Behrens men. Right, Tate?"

Tate gave a lazy grin and reached his arms up to his father. Jack swooped down and lifted Tate up. The little boy nestled his head on Jack's shoulder. "Rock me, Daddy."

"You are a little old for that, bud," Jack muttered in his ear as if he was embarrassed for Molly to hear. The boy was still little compared to his dad. His feet only dangled midthigh on Jack, and his head was completely tucked beneath his father's cheek.

Tate lifted his head and wagged his eyebrows. "Maybe you could swing me instead? I think that would do the trick." His voice grew high-pitched. Even Molly could tell that he was using his charm to prolong bedtime. "Pleeease."

Jack narrowed his eyes. "Sneaky guy." Tate buried his face in Jack's shoulder and belly laughed.

Molly wanted to reach out and rub Tate's back—an instinct she had never had before in her entire life. "You all feel free. I was just going to bed—"

Jack let out an uneasy laugh. "Bud, it's well past your bedtime. Let's just go—"

"Oh, sorry—I didn't mean to encourage..." Molly really knew nothing about parenting, kids or a bedtime. She was an architect: working in the wee hours was a skill she learned in her studios at Notre Dame.

Tate's head shot up. "No, Miss Molly. You swing with us." Tate squirmed out of Jack's arms and plodded on the floor. "C'mon." He scrambled up into the swing and patted his hands on either side of him. Molly shrank back, shaking her head and grabbing the door handle.

Jack sat beside Tate. "I want you to try and go to sleep, Tate. It's been a long day. We can only swing if you promise to try." Tate nodded, climbed into his lap and circled his arms around Jack's neck again.

Jack locked eyes with her. "C'mon, Miss Molly." The corners of his mouth twitched, and his eyes lit with humor. "There's plenty of room." He patted beside him.

Tate swiveled to give her a full-on smile, then rested his head on his dad's chest.

Reluctantly, Molly sat on the swing. Jack began to push off the porch with his boots, and they fell into a slow swinging motion. The familiar old squeal of the chains on the eye hooks accompanied the constant chatter of cicadas in the distance.

Molly lifted her fuzzy slippers out in front of her then crossed her ankles, trying to avoid disrupting the rhythm. Other than that, she was uncertain how to be in this situation at all. Sitting next to her ex-boyfriend on the same swing they had spent time together, the same spot of their first kiss, and the same porch of their breakup. Molly wanted to slink away and leave all this weirdness behind, like a garden snake shedding its skin. Yeah, her nerves were begging her to crawl out of her skin right now.

"Miss Molly? Do you know any good bedtime stories?" A drowsy question arose from the bundle on Jack's chest.

"Not really."

"My daddy tells the best ones. About—"

"Let me guess…superheroes?" Molly smirked.

Tate popped his head up and with the most genuine look of surprise exclaimed, "How did you know?"

"I think we are easy reads, Tate," Jack mused. Tate furrowed his brow and stared at his dad. "Spending a day with us, she understands that superheroes are pretty important."

Tate nodded. "Especially since *we* are superheroes." He pushed his face up and kissed Jack's nose.

Molly's nerves gave way to a flood of warmth. She'd never seen anything so sweet.

"Yes. Yes, we are." Jack flashed an apologetic look at Molly. Tate snuggled back down, and Jack pressed his cheek against Tate's brown hair. The boy's dark lashes were visible, but his face was buried in Jack's T-shirt.

"You're a good daddy." Molly nudged Jack gently with her elbow, unable to resist voicing such an understatement. Jack's cheek mussed Tate's hair as he smiled at her.

Molly looked away quickly. A whole different set of nerves engaged: old fluttery ones that never once calmed down all those days on this porch swing.

Tate made a hiccup sound, then let out a soft, jagged breath. Molly spied him out of her periphery.

Jack kissed the top of Tate's head, then leaned his head back. "He's out."

"Really? That was fast," Molly said in a hushed tone.

"I knew when he asked to be rocked he was ready to go." Humor laced his own whisper. "Every muscle is relaxed. He just grew a couple pounds heavier." He nestled the little boy closer to him. "He hasn't been rocked to sleep since he was little. Actually, since we were here the weeks after Brittany's passing."

"Looks like swinging does the trick." Molly fiddled with the blanket in her arms. She asked, "Does he remember…being rocked?"

"He knows it from a picture I have of Brittany rocking him. She said her favorite place was the rocker with Tate snuggled in her arms." He glanced around the porch, then set his soft eyes directly on her. "This is one of my favorite places too, this swing." A half smile grew beneath a simmering gaze.

Molly forced herself to look away. "Come on, Jack. That was eons ago."

"Right. Eons." He sighed. "So much time has passed."

Molly only nodded. She set her tiptoes on the floor and matched his rhythm. They rocked the swing together. She leaned into him. "I am so sorry about all you've been through. Sounds like Brittany was a great mom."

Jack locked his hands together on Tate's back. "I've never seen a woman so ready to be a mom. Brittany shone bright with an expectant mother's glow," he chuckled. "She taught me a lot about being a parent. Wonder how much more I would have learned if she hadn't left so soon." Jack squinted out into the darkness beyond the porch.

Molly followed his gaze, wondering what she might have learned if her mom had stuck around. Maybe it was good that she'd left when she did. All the tension and turmoil depleted enough so Molly could at least make room to dream.

"Remember when you begged me to let you tutor me?" Jack turned his head toward her with a smoldering look.

Molly gaped. "So not true. You begged me to tutor you. I only did it because Mr. Thatcher guilted me."

"What? I doubt that." He rolled his eyes.

"It's true. He asked in the name of Raider pride." Molly giggled and rolled her eyes too. "High-school football was pretty important around here. Still is, I am sure." Jack continued to look at her with disbelief. "You think you were so irresistible that I just had to say yes?" She raised her brow and mustered up the sassiest look possible.

"Well...yeah." His eyes flashed with that same cockiness that Molly had weirdly been attracted to back then. His light brown eyes shimmered with amusement, and the corners of his mouth threatened a full-on grin. "I was pretty stoked when you agreed, I must admit." He diverted his attention to the little boy sleeping against him.

Molly could hardly believe that high-school Jack had been so smitten. Well, at least she thought it hard to believe now. Her memory always replayed the needy, heartbroken girl longing to chase after the aloof dream guy. "That really does surprise me, Jack."

"Of course it does." He carefully stood. Tate's little feet dangling. "I wasn't one to wear my emotions on my sleeve. That's something else I've learned from Brittany. It's okay to show it."

Molly rose too. Her bundled blanket was much less cozy than Jack's armful. "Sounds like Brittany was a smart woman." She reached out her arm, pushed past her own resistance and rubbed Tate's back. "Wish I could have met her."

Jack whispered goodnight and headed down the steps to his truck which was parked a little farther away than usual. Molly slipped through the screen door, thinking how he probably parked there so he wouldn't disturb anyone.

This was certainly not the same guy in Molly's dreams from yesteryear. Somehow, Jack was proving to Molly that Polk Center wasn't just a place she'd hoped to forget but a place where memories might need to be corrected. Certain enemies might actually be a little more like superheroes.

Chapter Twelve

The next few days were busy and productive. And surprisingly entertaining with Tate around offering one-liners and enthusiasm for the simplest chores. Once Jack arrived to help in the afternoons, Molly spent most of the time forcing herself to pay attention to Tate, Gertie and her own task at hand, more than snooping around the place to find out where Jack was. But inevitably, they bumped into each other, and she caught herself, more than once, completely amused by his playful banter and dashing smiles. Remaining focused and diligent became an art form she'd forgotten back in Chicago—or maybe packed away in one of the many bins stacked up in the storage shed.

Only at night when the house grew quiet could Molly's mind tune into the world of architecture. Although, the still rooms without a little boy or a handsome farmer became stagnant, their lack of life too obvious.

In the very quietest moments, bits of the conversation she overheard while Gertie and Jack were on the porch last Sunday grew static around her clarity. Guilt began to grow as Austin Farm expanded toward the future without Grandad around.

About five hundred Thursdays had passed since Molly had last ventured into Polk Center's town square, and today was the Thursday to end her streak of staying away. Gran had taken the initiative and set up an appointment with the new real estate agent. As they turned onto Main Street, the sycamores were no less tall than what Molly remembered. They were huge, offering dapples of light across the lush green lawn and spotty shadows on the white gazebo at the very center of the square. Patriotic bunting hung from the gazebo trim, no doubt left over from the annual July Fourth parade. If Molly remembered correctly, the flags would be replaced with spirited Polk Center Raiders flags during high-school football season. She preferred the red, white, and blue. Molly could admire that without hesitation.

"So the general store is now an ice-cream parlor?" She pulled into a space along the north side of the square.

"Yep. A new grocery store opened down on First and hired Burt as grocery manager. His son and daughter-in-law spent that spring liquidating inventory in the old store, then remodeled in time for last day of school celebrations. Best hot fudge sundae I've ever had."

"Wow, that's saying something. I know how much you love ice cream." Molly giggled and admired the rustic sign that boasted the name Sugar in the Round, underscored by an old-fashioned metal scoop. "Cute name."

Molly breathed in deep, marveling at the change. Change was good. People here moved on, just like she had. Her nerves settled as she followed Gran along the sidewalk, observing the pizza place that was once Jack's dad's restaurant. The place of her first date with Jack. She diverted her attention to the real estate office.

When they entered the glass door to Blackwell Realty, Molly's aversion to this trip in the first place was justified. She couldn't find Blackwell in her memory bank, but now, seeing the slicked-back hair and the broad forehead peeking above the cubicle behind the receptionist's desk, she remembered.

Frank Blackwell. The guy Mom had dated after the divorce. Even though Molly was only seven and had had enough life between the old trailer and her loft apartment to not care one bit about facing this man, the longing in her heart for the woman who Frank had dated—albeit briefly—was uninvitedly flaring up.

"Gran, do you know who that—" Molly bit her tongue. No, Gran did not know. Back when Mom and Frank dated, Molly hardly saw her grandparents. Mom hadn't been speaking to her parents because she was upset that Dad was still working for Grandad after the divorce. Those few months were a blur. Molly hadn't thought about her wood-paneled bedroom or Mom's late nights out while Dad came over and slept on the couch so Molly wouldn't be alone.

The receptionist hung up the phone. "Well, hi there. Can I help you?"

"Yes, I called about putting my property on the market." Gran fiddled with the clasp of her purse. The long wrinkles along her cheek had always been there, but they pronounced sadness more this day than Molly had noticed. "Been fifty years coming," Gran admitted on a sputtering laugh.

Molly rubbed her back. "Maybe we should do this another day?" Out of the thousands of agents in the greater

Des Moines area, they had plenty of other choices be-sides Frank Blackwell.

Frank walked into the lobby. "Farm north of town right?" He pointed a finger at Gran, bouncing an eager gaze between the two women.

Gran sniffled. "Yes. How did you know?"

Frank pushed his bottom lip up, overtaking his upper lip. "I read about Rob in the *Daily Banner*. I am so sorry for your loss."

"Thank you." Gran's voice wobbled. "Well, guess you were expecting us sooner or later."

Frank let out a nervous chuckle. "Not exactly." He now stared at Molly, arching his eyebrows. "Didn't think I'd ever see an Austin gal in here, or a Jansen." He cleared his throat. "My, Molly, you've grown up."

Molly's blood was pumping so thick in her ears, her head was going to explode. The man had been nice enough when he'd come over to eat dinner with them. But Molly didn't recall ever talking to him. He'd been consumed with Mom. And Mom, likewise. She shud-dered and looked down at her watch.

"Oh, you remember my Molly." Gran brushed her hand along the back of Molly's hair. "She's grown up into an accomplished architect."

Molly just raised her brow, then grabbed a brochure on a table beneath the window.

"Wow, that's great." Frank rocked back on his heels. Perhaps he noticed Molly's discomfort. He clicked his tongue and blurted, "Let me get you a welcome folder. Be right back."

After Frank gave his spiel, Molly was eager to get out of there. But just as she turned to follow Gran, Frank grabbed her arm and spoke low. "Hey, how's your mom? Looked her up when I got back in town but…" He shrugged his shoulders.

Molly bristled. "She's fine."

She stepped into the afternoon sun, imagining her cold shoulder outmatched the air conditioner in the small office. Oh well. Impressing her mom's ex-boyfriend was the least of her concerns. But pretending she knew how her mom was doing was not great.

Deflated, she hooked arms with Gran and said, "I really think we will have better luck with someone who's experienced with acreages. Frank lists mainly condos and double-wides."

"I agree." Gran patted her hand. "And maybe somewhere a little outside of Polk Center. Having to accept condolences at every turn will not make this any easier." She lifted her shoulders and released them with a huff. "I think I see why you stayed away, my dear."

Molly cringed internally, squeezing out the unease that had inched just a tad closer from the back of her mind. She had shoved it away with each night's sleep, consumed her thoughts with the Behrens while they were around, and then bathed in whatever creative energy she could pour out at night. But Gran's solidarity in avoiding Polk Center was unexpected. Molly caught the glint from the old ice-cream scoop, taking it as a wink to cheer up her grandmother. Or, at least, treat her to one of her favorite things. "Let's get some ice cream."

"Before dinner?"

"Living on the edge, Gran. And I'm needing a little sugar therapy. How 'bout you?"

"Yes, ma'am." She laughed. "Hey, how did you know Frank? He's only been here since last fall."

"Nah, he was around when I was younger. He was a

plumber Mom hired." Molly left it at that. He had been a plumber back then. That was true.

"Gran!" A familiar voice called from behind them. Tate ran down the sidewalk from the pizza place. Jack was pushing through the door holding a pizza box.

Tate crashed into Gran, wrapping his arms around her thigh.

"Oh, Super Tate! You are a force to be reckoned with." Gran patted his back. "Been so long since we last saw you."

"Nah, I was just at your house." Missing the sarcasm, he put his hand over very serious eyes to block out the sun. "Remember?"

Gran nodded, and Molly laughed.

"Pizza, the dinner of champions." Jack approached with his usual full-teeth smile. He glanced over at the real estate office. The smile faded a smidge. "Making headway?"

Gran's exasperated breath lifted her bangs. Jack's gaze skipped to Molly. His dimples lingered with a more subtle smile than before.

Molly scrunched her nose and shook her head quickly. "We're getting ice cream for dinner, if that tells you anything."

"Ice cream for dinner?" Tate guffawed. "Da-ad!"

"Oops, sorry." Molly gave an apologetic grin to Jack. "We'll let you all get to your pizza."

Tate ran up to Molly and grabbed her hand. "I'm going with you."

Molly froze and just stared down at his little fingers clasping hers. "Aw, Tate. I don't think you can leave your dad to eat that whole pizza all by himself."

"Yes, I can. He's got a big stomach." Tate began to tug her toward the ice-cream shop.

"Tate Behrens," Jack managed to say as they all tried to refrain from laughing.

"It's okay, Dad. I don't mind."

"Tate!"

Tate dropped his shoulders, looked up at Molly and said, "You aren't fast enough, Miss Molly."

"I think your dad would have caught us even if we ran."

"Maybe. But he's a gentleman. He'd have let you win." Tate reached up on his tiptoes and motioned for her to bend down. She did so, and he whispered, "And we'd have gotten ice cream then."

Tate released her hand and walked over to his dad. The superhero cape bounced along his back. Molly couldn't help but melt a little.

"Looks like you just gave up on a sneaky partner-in-crime," Jack spoke to Molly and patted Tate's head.

Molly lifted her hands in surrender. "I am no fun at all. Sorry, Tate." She winked at the little boy who stood with his arms crossed. "Before I leave, we'll have to convince your dad to let us get ice cream, okay?"

His eyes lit up, and he nodded.

"See you all tomorrow." Jack dipped his chin then turned to his truck.

Gran and Molly said goodbye and headed to Sugar in the Round.

"My, Molly Jansen, you just made a date with a four-year-old," Gran teased and nudged her.

Molly chuckled and looked over her shoulder. What was she thinking making a promise like that? She'd probably not have time to finish painting the kitchen, let alone take a child she hardly knew on an ice-cream date. Yet, little Tate just had a way of drumming up joy these past few days, without even trying.

Jack jogged around the front of the truck after helping Tate inside. He slowed when he caught her staring. She spun around and walked faster, trying to convince herself that the suspicious flutters in her tummy were only because hot fudge, Oreo topping and chocolate ice cream waited beneath that metal ice-cream scoop.

They went inside, ordered and sat down in the big picture window. Molly's fluttering became lead wings crashing to the bottom of her stomach. She was on display in the very center of Polk Center. Frank Blackwell headed to his Ford Taurus and took off around the square. A few moms with young kids in tow were crossing over to the playground on the other side of the gazebo. Molly chided herself for caring so much about what the people passing by might think of her. Nobody was looking—or caring—that she was back. That was a comforting thought, until a couple of familiar faces opened the glass door. And she was certain that they were speaking *about her* in low voices after throwing a couple of wondering glances her way as they went up to order.

The childhood scent of waffle cones, ice cream and warming caramel was hardly comforting. Her stomach twisted with a sickly feeling.

Couldn't she just wear a sign saying that she hadn't followed in her mom's wild footsteps like everyone presumed? Molly was not like any of the horrible names they had mocked her with when Mom's shenanigans had raced through the Polk Center grapevine.

Molly was not her mother.

But nobody cared to know Molly then. And she really didn't feel like giving anyone second chances to get to know her now.

She looked over her shoulder to the spot where Jack had parked. He was gone. He did know her. She didn't really want him to. But because of Grandad, Jack Behrens not only knew the present-day Molly but understood the pain of her many losses and knew the whereabouts of her infamous mother.

The two familiar customers were ordering. If she remembered correctly, they had been a couple in high school. They seemed hardly grown up at all, except for the baby bump.

The woman slid a look just past Molly's forehead, as if she was nonchalantly looking out the window. Molly knew what was going on. It was the rumor mill scraping away the rust and figuring out how to churn again.

Molly-Moo was back. And Grandad wasn't here to protect or comfort. His wife sat across from her with a dozen new worry lines marking his absence.

If only Molly could have spent time with Grandad at his beloved farmhouse once more, instead of her grandparents always traveling to Illinois or meeting in the city. Polk Center had scared her away, but should she have let it keep her away from making more memories at Austin Farm? She looked over at Gran. How many of those worry lines were because of Molly and her stubbornness? How many had etched into Grandad's forehead from a granddaughter who'd left and never returned to his beloved farm?

Chapter Thirteen

All the way from the ice-cream parlor to the car to the turn down Jack's drive, Gran held a plastic box in her lap. Inside, an ice cream cone sat upside down, decorated with a superhero logo in frosting on colorful ice cream. Molly couldn't resist buying it for Tate, since she couldn't guarantee that date she'd suggested. What if the house stuff distracted her from follow-through? She just couldn't bear letting the kid down. If anyone knew what it felt like to get stood up, it was Molly Jansen. Not really as a young adult but as a nine-year-old, a ten-year-old…all the way through her teen years when Mom promised one thing but failed to stick to her word.

After Molly put the car in Park, she took the box from Gran, hopped out and walked up the uneven sidewalk. She peered over her shoulder. Gran was in the car playing on her phone, completely unaware of the underlying reason Molly had insisted they stop by Jack's. It was not just about an ice-cream delivery.

A gloomy cloud had been accumulating in Molly's heart during those quiet moments these past few days, and the only person who might help was Jack Behrens.

She couldn't mention anything to Gran. The real estate office proved that Gran could not manage a good long look backward. She was still raw, not even wanting condolences right now. Grandad's funeral was less than a week ago, after all.

Surprisingly, Jack might be her only chance for some peace. Or at least insight.

His split-level house was like most houses in an aging Midwest neighborhood, but it sat on a small acreage off the same road as Austin Farm. Yellow siding, black shutters and a shallow, sloped roof with one center gable above the front door. She could make out the narrow foyer through the sidelight. Stairs led up to the main living area. Along a wall beside the stairs was a coatrack with Carhartt jackets, a tiny raincoat and, of course, a superhero cape. She knocked on the front door, noticing the plethora of shoes and boots beneath the coats.

As Jack bounded down the steps on the other side of the window, she stepped back, her neck and cheeks heating at her nosiness. Molly cast a look to the car where Gran was still consumed with her phone, then stared hard at the cold box in her hands as the door opened.

His cap was backward, a bath towel was flung over his shoulder, and his white T-shirt had runaway suds along his waistline.

"Bath time?" Molly smirked, but thought his appearance was adorable.

Jack looked down, then back up. A smile grew wide and bright on his shadowy face. Those dimples were magnets for Molly's own smile to scatter into undeniable amusement. "Just finished. The superhero is getting into his pajamas."

"I won't keep you—" Molly scrunched her nose and

looked down at the ice cream cone. "Wanted to drop this off to Tate. Couldn't help but think of him and—"

Jack opened the door wider and stepped aside. "Why don't you come in and give it to him?"

"Oh no," Molly nearly snapped. She pushed her chin up apologetically. "Sorry. I just... I also wanted to ask you a question. Alone."

Jack's eyes widened. He took the towel and tossed it on the stairs then stepped out into the early evening. "Of course. What is it, Mol?" He cupped her elbow, concern crinkling just beneath the baseball cap's strap. He pressed his lips together and fluttered his eyelashes. "Molly. I mean, Molly." His hand dropped. Molly's shoulders dropped involuntarily.

She breathed in deep, staring only at the box in her hands. Cedar, mint and baby shampoo filled the space. The handsome-farmer-slash-single-dad cologne. Molly would expect that baby wash would just kill all the jitters that frenzied more and more as she spent time with Jack. But it did the exact opposite. Jack Behrens was an excellent father, proving he was so much more the man than the guy who she'd longed for but could never convince to give his heart completely to her.

Jack stepped closer. His athletic socks slid into view. "Everything okay?"

She looked up. He was so close. His eyes caught all the light above and around them, the amber specks in his brown pools highlighted by the afternoon sunshine. But instead of admiring the countryside, he stayed focused on her.

"It's fine. I just... I—" Molly volleyed her gaze between his eyes, nose to mouth. She hadn't been this near someone in a very long time—besides a hug from Gran...or Grandad.

Grandad.

She stepped back and cleared her throat. "Grandad."

"Huh?"

"I know he bragged on me all the time. You and every Polk Center resident over fifty has said so." She looked off toward a fallow field across the road. "But what about disappointment? Was he ever sad that I wasn't around?" Molly caught her tears with the back of her hand, the ice-cream box saved by Jack's quick catch. "Sorry."

"It's okay. I am going to get this in the freezer. Just a sec." He ran inside but poked his head out again. "Don't leave." Molly nodded.

The screen door shut behind him, and Molly was alone. She sniffled and wiped away the rest of the run-away tears. Gran was squinting at her from the car. Molly gave her a thumbs-up and then held up her pointer finger signaling just a little longer. Molly gripped the thin metal railing and faced the sprawling lawn between the house and the road.

She should have come alone. But that would give off all sorts of mixed messages—especially to the heart slamming around in her chest.

Jack returned, his hat turned the right way round. He stood beside her, gripping the rail just next to her own hands. "Molly, he thought the world of you. Not one negative word."

Molly crossed her arms. "I missed so much." She shook her head and inhaled a jagged breath. "While Gran and Grandad always put my wishes first, making the five-hour trek to me, or meeting me in Des Moines,

I never thought that one day I would return to Polk Center and realize all the chances I might regret."

"Chances?"

"Chances to make more memories at Austin Farm with Grandad around. Chances to get to know some people…old friends who've grown up to be pretty great."

"Hmm, my super sense tells me you're talking about yours truly." He chuckled and nudged her with an elbow.

She rolled her eyes and tightened her ponytail. "Really, though, did he seem sad that I always made them come to me?"

"Molly, look at me." Jack was now turned toward her. She faced him. He swiped his hat off his head and twisted it in his hands. "There was not one ounce of negativity that came from that man's mouth when it came to you." He searched her face as if he hunted for palpable belief in what he said.

"I am not so sure I can trust that to be true." All the thoughts she'd tried to avoid these past few days bubbled to the surface.

"Why?"

A cynical snigger escaped her lips. "Now, there's an age-old answer to that. I am my mother's daughter, after all. You've filled in the gaps of yet another Jansen woman who abandoned Austin Farm."

Jack placed a firm hand on her arm. "Molly Jansen, you can't be serious? If anything, Rob thought the world of you because you proved to yourself, to him, to all of Polk Center, that Molly Jansen was her own person with an amazing dream. You did everything right, Molly."

Another, less pronounced cynical burst left her lips. "And Mom did the exact opposite."

"Not your burden to bear."

Molly glanced over at the screen door. "Well, not entirely true. You know, moms are pretty integral to a kid. No matter what kind of mom. You've said that before." That gloomy cloud darkened. "Maybe I was just another reminder of the daughter they lost. Come to think of it, might have been easy to not miss me."

"That's absurd, Molly."

"It's okay. I just needed to double-check I did the right thing. It sounds like I absolutely did." She spun around, her eyes now stinging, her heart thumping, not because of the cute ex behind her but because of her own embarrassment.

She shouldn't have come here.

Even if Grandad had missed her, there was not one thing she could do about it. Just like her mother, Molly *had* left Polk Center for good, even if it meant losing out on all that time with some of the best folks in the world: Rob and Gertie Austin. Now, the place that held whatever memories were made before her great abandonment was being sold off to the highest bidder. Regret, remorse or whatever seemed to keep haunting her in this Iowa zip code were distractions that she needed to lay to rest. Molly was as helpless as the little girl who wondered if she would sleep in an empty trailer all alone every night of her eighth year on earth.

Digging up assurance that Grandad wasn't disappointed in her was never going to happen. Making up for lost time was never going to happen. She needed to move forward with the plan.

This return trip to Polk Center couldn't end soon enough.

* * *

Jack watched Molly and Gertie leave his driveway followed by a cloud of dust from the gravel road. He leaned up against the rail and tried to breathe away the old grief that welled up inside him as he heard Molly's new grief debilitate her peace.

Tate pushed open the screen door, his bath towel tied around his shoulders, and his hair slicked back like Clark Gable.

"Hey, little man." Jack squatted and held his arms out. Tate tumbled into them with a giant bear hug around Jack's neck.

"Dad, I used your comb. Do you think I look grown-up?" He pulled away and fanned his hand along his wet hair.

Jack laughed. "You sure do." Oh, how Brittany would have loved to see Tate at this age! He wasn't just a toddler with high-pitched squeals but a little boy perfecting an amazing sense of humor and cultivating a joy for life despite his obstacles.

Brittany would have made the most of every moment with photos, then reliving it in her special way of storytelling. Jack would have listened happily, contentedly, admiring his wife as much as she admired Tate.

"Hey, let me get a picture. You look great." Jack pulled out his phone and snapped a picture of the posing Tate.

"Let me see!"

"Here, all grown-up," Jack said. "But not too grown-up for an upside-down ice cream cone, I suspect?"

Tate's eyes rounded, and his mouth dropped.

"Miss Molly brought a treat for you. It's in the freezer."

Tate spun on his foot and flung open the screen door. "Is Miss Molly here? I wanna show her how handsome I am."

Jack stood up from squatting and rubbed the back of his neck, calling out, "She's gone now. I can send her the picture." Or send it to Gertie. Jack didn't have Molly's number.

Tate called from the kitchen. "No, I want to surprise her on our date."

"Well, I think that's why she brought you a cone. She's not sure she'll be able to take you."

Jack opened the door and bounded up the stairs to the main level. Tate stood in the center of the kitchen with the plastic box in his hands. He just stared at it.

"What's up? Do you not like it?"

"Nah. I just wanted to go with Miss Molly." He dragged his feet over to the kitchen counter and climbed onto a stool then started opening the box.

Jack handed him a spoon. "She's a pretty nice lady, huh?"

"She is. Doesn't talk to me like I am a baby. I like that." He dug into the colorful ice cream and shoved a spoonful with candy eyes into his mouth. Finishing his bite and digging in his spoon for another, he said, "And she's pretty too. Don't you think?" Tate slid a sideways glance to Jack, his dimple appearing among his freckles.

Jack narrowed his eyes and headed to the sink to finish up some dishes. But mostly, he was trying to reason away the stampede in his chest at Tate's sneaky question. Was he not only growing a sense of humor but matchmaking skills too?

If Tate only knew that Molly Jansen had snagged Jack's heart once, long ago. If Molly only knew that she was no longer in a shadow of her past, but she was shining bright enough for Rob to look down and smile.

Jack caught a glimpse at his favorite picture of Brittany, a couple weeks after she finished chemo. They had eaten dinner at a new restaurant in downtown Des Moines, and if he remembered correctly, they began conspiring to take a trip to Disney World for Tate's birthday. But with the next check-up came the worst news of their lives—the treatment hadn't worked, and the cancer had spread—and all traveling plans went out the window.

Well, until there seemed to be nothing left to do, and Brittany suggested they make the most of her time left. She wanted to try the trip. To travel, even though she felt horrible. Jack couldn't imagine it. He refused to give in. They spent their last weeks at home, then the hospital, bracing for an unwanted future.

Just like Molly, Jack couldn't shake the missed chances once Brittany had passed. His decision to stay home was made out of hurt and fear, but he hadn't been able to conceive of the loss that might come with it. Losing some magical last moments at Disney to dark days of hunkering down in these four walls? The regret had been enormous.

Gertie helped Jack during those first bouts of guilt. He couldn't have known, and he had acted in Brittany's best interest. Now Jack could see that Molly was putting a whole lot of guilt on her own shoulders. And he completely understood the temptation to do so.

Jack wiped his hands on the dish towel and pulled out his phone.

Hey Gertie. Molly's regretting some missed chances with Rob. I know you are wise to these kinds of guilt trips. You helped me once. Thought you would want to know.

Jack sat next to Tate while he ate his ice cream. His little boy wasn't as enthusiastic about such a fun treat when the chance of a fun memory with Molly at the ice-cream shop had just got dashed with Jack's honesty.

If he was honest with himself, he was a little bummed too. For Molly's sadness and guilt. Also, he was bummed that she was not sticking around but leaving their lives as quickly as she once left town long ago.

Chapter Fourteen

On the drive home, Gran had asked if everything was okay, and Molly had given her best *Just fine* then admitted she was reminiscing about Grandad when Gran pointed out her teary eyes. They cranked up the radio and listened to old country, Molly singing along to make sure the conversation would not continue.

That evening, after watching reruns with Gran while they went through old files in the dining room, Molly decided to forget working for a while and just get some rest. Had she ever felt so unsettled with the work on her desk? Her passion for it had dulled on Jack's porch. Did she follow a dream to a fault?

When she finally headed upstairs after saying goodnight to Gran, Molly wondered if sleep would come at all as her mind nearly exploded with debriefing all she had felt—and said—during that meltdown with Jack. Her tossing and turning was interrupted by the hallway light.

Gran approached her doorway. "You still awake, dear?"

"Yep. Is something the matter?"

"Just wanted to say thank-you again. Grandad's no

doubt beaming right now." Gran's silhouette was framed by the amber glow from the hallway. She was petite, more than Molly remembered her to be.

Molly pushed herself up on her elbows. "Do you think so? I mean, I should have come back before…don't you think? I would have had more time with him…"

"Shoulda, woulda?" Gran scoffed. "You are an Austin girl. *Can* and *will* are more our go-to words. Don't lie there regretting—"

"How do you know I am doing that?" Molly smirked. "Maybe I am thinking about real estate fees and finally fixing that newel on the banister?" She chuckled softly, thinking how much lighter she'd feel if that was true.

Gran came over and sat at the foot of her bed. She patted Molly's feet. "I couldn't help but see your obvious distress at Jack's. You think my phone was that interesting while you two had a heart-to-heart out there? All I know how to do on it is play a silly word game, send texts…and receive them." She pushed her chin up, and on a sigh admitted, "Jack filled me in."

"What?" Heat flooded Molly's cheeks. She suddenly felt like the girl sitting at the front of the class, while everyone whispered about her mom the day after she was arrested for public intoxication. Nobody asked Molly about it, just took it upon themselves to gab away. "Why didn't you ask me yourself?"

"Why didn't you tell me how you were feeling?" She arched a brow and clicked her tongue, hurt glancing her eyes. "You said you were just reminiscing about Grandad when I asked if everything was okay."

Molly lifted her brow in surrender. "I didn't want to upset you, Gran. But I'd rather you have not gone to Jack."

"Jack is one of the good guys. I didn't text him, honey. He texted me."

"He did?"

"He was very concerned for you. He understands how regret can become a monster. The first few months after Brittany passed, most of my job was talking him out of all his shame in what he couldn't fix and what he thought he had messed up during his time left with her."

Molly mumbled, "He's been filling in the gaps around here a little too much."

"Much needed, actually." Gran smiled. "Another thing an Austin knows how to do is give space when it's needed—and sometimes that leaves things unsaid that need to be said."

"And sometimes they just leave. Period. Never to return. As far as Grandad knows, I am just like…Mom." Molly hung her head, loaded with remorse. She'd never felt so close to Mom as she did in this writhing realization that she'd followed in her footsteps.

Gran gasped. She shot up from the bed and loomed over Molly as much as the petite lady could. Hooking her finger under Molly's chin she tilted her head up. "Hear me now. Not once did we think you were wrong in leaving."

"But I could have come back every once in a while."

"And we could have spoken up in town more. The gossipmongers weren't just in your high school, Mol. We ran away to the farm just like you ran away to Chicago. The distance is different, but the running away part is the same."

Molly searched Gran's face through globs of tears. Gran was as serious as a farmer on the first day of harvest. Unflinching brow and piercing eyes that demanded agreement. Molly took her hand from her chin, held it gently then lifted an arm to hook around Gran's neck in a heartfelt hug. She whispered, "Thank you for always being there for me."

Gran squeezed back. "Love you, Molly-Moo. Now get some rest." She pulled away. "Let's enjoy our time left here, you hear?"

Molly nodded. Gran left her room, plodded down the stairs, then shut off the hall light. The shadows of the dark hallway and her familiar room gave plenty of room for Molly to ponder all Gran had said.

Just like Gran did not want her last days here to be filled with sadness, Molly could not let her last memories of this home be overwhelmed by regret. She rolled over and searched her mind for anything that brought joy. Her surroundings tugged her into dreamy moments with Jack, just as if she were a teen again. She barreled past them to her unfinished conceptual drawings. She closed her eyes. As she considered the next spaces she would design, she was annoyed with the constant distraction peeking from the edge of her locked-away thoughts. A sun-kissed farmer who redeemed old memories with sweet dreams.

The next morning, Molly woke up to her shoulders declaring they would never participate in house remodeling again. Pain radiated across her back and underarms. She groaned as she flipped over to spy the weak light barely seeping through the blinds. Taking care as she turned back over, she winced and glanced at her phone: 5:20 a.m.

It was early yet.

Any other day, she would hit Snooze. But she checked

her heart after last night's talk with Gran. Sorrow was still there, but mostly she was thankful. Thankful for Gran who always had a way of pouring wisdom into a situation. And no matter how much she disliked Jack's interference in her personal matters, she was grateful he cared enough to reach out to Gran in the first place.

Lingering on Jack a little too long, Molly caught herself twirling her hair around her finger and smiling for no reason in particular. She sat up quickly and cleared her throat.

Work!

She forced her mind to shift to her project. Checking her heart once more, she was especially pleased that her desire to work was rekindled. Today, she would reward her grunt work these past few days with dream work this morning. The thought of that beautiful future residence on the bank of the Mississippi was a balm to all her aches and pains and a pick-me-up for a short night's sleep. She was ready to delve into the order of structure, design, beauty. Molly needed to recommit herself to the steady pace that had settled from the typical Jansen girl's selfish running away. No matter how much she berated herself for doing the exact same thing as her mom— leaving, never to return—Molly decided to trust Gran, like usual. Molly hadn't left in a bad way. She'd left to pursue a dream, not to abandon her family. All she had was this moment. Whatever time she missed out on with Grandad could never be regained. But she could make the most of what Grandad had left behind.

Molly grabbed her robe and slippers and piled her hair in a bun as she crept downstairs. Instead of working at that old desk, though, she had a better idea. One that fueled her desire to work here—in this place—or rather, just a few steps outside where Austin roots sprawled wide and deep with creativity, tenacity and simplicity. *Simplicity* meant something different here in Polk Center than it did in the big city. Simplicity was not clean precision but raw materials. It was not straight edges but rough and ready tools. The ruggedness of a farm workshop was a place of simplicity because it was the very bed of potential—the foundation upon which ideas bloomed into function.

Molly stacked her laptop and notepad in her arms. The pungent smell of fresh paint lured her to the kitchen, and she admired the light grey walls that were finally finished. The coffeepot was as cold as the John Deere engine outside, and for now, Molly would just let it stay that way, surprising herself by passing up her caffeine intake.

Unlocking the back door carefully, she stepped into the cool, damp air. Rich soil and dew-soaked corn leaves awakened the dormant farm girl inside her. She shook away the sputtering remorse left over from yesterday and nearly jogged across to the garage, ready to set up at the workbench.

Molly whispered a prayer of thanksgiving for Austin Farm, her life with Grandad and her amazing Gran. She then began to work like Grandad would have taught her: focused, steady and determined with a knife-sharpened pencil on a piece of paper, beneath a picture-perfect view of a cornfield. All the leftover sawdust from the last of Austin creations filled her nostrils with her very first inspiration for creativity—Grandad. Molly was certain she was exactly where she needed to be.

* * *

"Gran's light's off," Tate said from the back seat as Jack pulled into the Austin driveway.

"It's still early, bud. We didn't get much sleep last night, so I thought I would work on Grandad's garage till Gran wakes up." He peered in the rearview mirror. Tate looked tired. They went ahead and used the vest around five this morning, since they were both up, anyway.

The window was still dark when Jack had hooked up the hoses and turned on Tate's favorite show. Starting before the sun was up had been reminiscent of many mornings with Brittany armoring up for a gallant fight against cystic fibrosis. Until her own fight began to wane. Brittany had been a morning person. Rarely did Tate do his vest past seven back then. The first morning she slept in had Jack on his knees begging God to redeem her tired body with healing. Didn't happen—and now Jack prayed in constant tension for his boy. Half with fierce expectancy that God would protect him, and half with doubt that he was being heard at all. Yet, Jack was determined to pray because that's what Brittany would do. Besides, he wasn't so sure that his discernment was up to par these days. Not with the stress of Rob's death and now his uncertain career path.

Jack put the truck in Park and pulled out his phone. He'd sent an email to a seed company late last night after his sister texted that she would be available for Tate next week. The sheer relief of knowing that Tate had a secure place to go once his work was done at the Austins' pushed him to do the unthinkable. Inquire about an office job close by.

The idea of being bound to a cubicle made his stomach sour, but the seed company was only twenty miles away, and his bills weren't doing anything but piling up. And after Tate had coughed throughout the night, Jack panicked that he would not be able to manage this on his own. Lisa was often reminding him about prescriptions and looking out for Tate when Jack was working. An office job was a small price to pay for keeping Tate healthy.

Of course, no email waited for him. It had only been five hours since he'd pressed Send.

He set his phone on the console and opened his door. The morning was cool. He relished the sixties temperature, knowing that it would heat up fast to the upper eighties. He poked his head in the truck and rested his chin on the back of the driver's seat. Tate was bouncing his heel with the song on his cartoon. No matter how crummy he felt, his little boy made the most of life.

"Hey, bud, I brought some blankets so you can sit on the porch swing with your iPad. I don't want you in the garage with all the dust."

"Can I stay in here? I am cozy." He glanced up and placed his hand on his water bottle in the cup holder of his booster seat. He offered a wide grin.

"You sure?"

Tate nodded, gave a thumbs-up, then went back to watching his show. His chest hitched inward a bit as he breathed.

Jack prayed again. His fierce expectancy eclipsing his doubt right now.

He headed down the flagstone path to the side door of the garage. The door was always unlocked, but it was never cracked open like it was now. Jack pushed it open, not sure if he would see a raccoon scavenging for food or a thief stealing Rob's designer tools. He did not expect to see Molly, standing at the workbench in a fuzzy pink robe, her hair in a bun adorned with a pencil. She didn't even notice him. Her attention was locked on her screen—her own career path.

"Hey there," he spoke softly, not wanting to scare her.

Yet, she jumped and whipped around. "Oh, hey!" She tightened her robe. "What time is it?" She glanced at her watch. "You are early."

"Rough night." He stuffed his hands in his pockets and took a few steps toward her. "I see you are getting some Rob Austin inspiration here."

She smiled. Did she just wake up looking so bright and refreshed? He rubbed his jaw, realizing he hadn't shaved. Rough and stubbly. Molly's smooth ivory skin was as vibrant as her gleaming eyes and rosy cheeks. Jack was certain his eyes were still bloodshot from his quick glance in the mirror a couple hours ago.

"Hey, thanks for listening to me yesterday." She crossed her arms over her waist. "Gran said you under-stand—more than I realized."

Jack dipped his chin with a quick nod. "Guilt seems to wiggle its way in when we lose someone."

Molly nibbled on her lip, turning her attention to the window. Her profile set him back to those days in high school when he'd catch himself staring at her across the classroom aisle. Now, she seemed to consider his words just like when they were supposed to brainstorm their next essay.

She turned to him and clarified. "*Some* loss comes with guilt. Not all." Her nostrils flared, and she rolled her eyes. "I really don't love that you know the latest about Mom. But, since you do, is it bad that my resent-ment has only grown since I found out?"

"Bad? Good? I don't know." Jack inhaled a choppy

breath. "Understandable, sure. I know resentment too. Wasn't too happy when my dad sold the restaurant and moved off in the middle of Brittany's diagnosis." He whistled and thought back further than his usual memory pit stops. "It was short-lived, though."

"How's that?"

"He had stuff of his own going on. Kinda made everything around him cloudy. Couldn't absorb my hurt when he was struggling too. I get it now." Jack kicked at the floor with his boot. "Mental health is like a storm. Hard to see through it…and definitely hard to empathize when you are just trying to stay above water."

His dad had confessed a bunch once he heard that Brittany was in the hospital for the last time. He had been struggling with depression, and the only way out was to step away from the demanding role as restaurant owner. He wasn't sleeping, hardly eating. Lots of dots were connected when Jack finally listened to him. At the time, Jack couldn't process too much, but they had a heartfelt conversation days after Brittany's funeral, and Jack finally let go of the resentment. "Everyone has battles that we can't see, I guess."

Molly just stared at him. She mumbled, "Mom showed hers often." She gave a sideways glance to the pegboard beside them, swiped her eyes, then cleared her throat and looked at him again. "Maybe you should quit your day job and become a counselor," she said in jest with a wink.

"Ah, that would be some practice. Set up shop in the cornfield. Like your special room. Only way I'd do it." He gritted his teeth thinking about the cubicle he might end up in.

"Ha! Don't steal my childhood fantasy, Mr. Behrens." She feigned a scowl. Then her whole face shone with excitement. "But wouldn't that be a super-cool office space? I'd come get counseling from the cornfield, anytime."

He leaned an elbow on the workbench and laughed. "Even in January?"

Molly pushed her lip up. "Mmm, you'd need to make yourself an igloo."

He wagged his head, unable to tone down his smile. "I forgot that about you."

She cocked her head. "What?"

"How great you are at turning something ordinary— like a cornfield—into something…exciting."

She shrugged her shoulders. "I've tried to tame it over the years. I get lost in the dream. Like…" her gaze skimmed the old garage "…I forget who I am…or was. I just focus on the dream. Maybe that's why I had that moment yesterday. I remembered who I was with Grandad and all that I had missed out on for the dream." Only a slight tug of her forehead signaled remnants of her sorrow. She breathed in deep and continued. "I never would have thought it, but you filling in the gap while I was gone has given me some peace with it all." She stepped forward but then hesitated. Her hands fell to her side. "Thank you." She only looked down at her slippers.

While she was talking in clichés about gaps, Jack fought the urge to close this very present gap between them. He wanted to wrap his arms around her, hold her close and absorb some of her imagination for grandness when it came to the mediocre—like a break from a career he loved. Suddenly, his mind slipped and holding her in his arms while working in that cubicle didn't seem so bad. Imagining a life with Molly around seemed to soothe the possibilities of a career not reaching its full potential. He opened his mouth to speak, uncertain of what to say. Afraid that his exhaustion was playing tricks on him.

Could Molly Jansen not only be here to fix up the farmhouse, but to also fill a forgotten gap in his heart?

Chapter Fifteen

The rest of the day, Tate was Molly's helper. They began
to fill boxes with knickknacks, and Tate learned how to
use the tape roller. He didn't seem as energetic as usual,
and he rattled as he breathed. Gran, Tate and Molly
headed to Des Moines and met with a real estate agent,
then ate lunch at a small deli. Tate barely ate his sandwich but was fine gobbling up a chocolate chip cookie.

"How are you feeling, Tater?" Gran asked as they
drove home. Molly glanced at the rearview mirror to
see Tate pressing his nose against the window.

"I'm okay." He spoke to the glass, his chest slightly
jerking with each breath. By the time they got to the
farm, Tate was drowsy, and Molly offered to carry him
inside. He was heavier than he looked. Her throat began
to close as she felt the warmth of his little arms around
her neck. She remembered a time when Dad brought
her up these porch steps. She'd clung onto him in the
same way that first day he decided that it was best for
his daughter to live with Gran and Grandad. Mom had
been leaving Molly home alone way too often, and the
final time Dad checked on Molly, there was an eviction

notice taped to the door. But Molly couldn't stay with Dad either since he worked on the farm with Grandad during the day and at a convenience store at night. So he had taken her to the Austin farmhouse. Molly's only true home.

Gran held open the door for Molly and said she was going to text Jack about Tate's symptoms. Molly crossed the room and lowered Tate to the couch. He was wheezing a bit. She hadn't noticed the dark circles around his eyes. At first glance, he seemed like a healthy boy with an enemy hidden deep in his lungs. But cystic fibrosis was showing itself today. His breathing wasn't great, and his face seemed fatigued. Without thinking, she brushed her hand across his forehead, and his eyes fluttered open.

She whispered, "Sorry for waking you."

"Thanks, Miss Molly." He turned over and fell asleep with his nose pressed against the back of the couch.

Gran handed Molly a blanket. "You're good with him."

Molly shook her head. "How can I be? I know nothing about kids."

"It's natural, I guess." Gran shrugged her shoulders. "Jack said to give him a breathing treatment when he wakes up."

Molly covered Tate with a quilt.

Her phone vibrated. She walked over to the desk, sat down and opened her text messages. Her assistant Lauren was asking about her concept, then mentioned Molly's competition had made several trips to the proposed property.

Molly blew a loose strand of hair away from her face, wondering if she should work right now. The sleeping breaths of the little boy behind her were steadier than her erratic pulse as she considered the competition was rev-ving up back in Chicago. Yet, something else bugged her.

Molly was thankful the assistant was just as competi-tive as her and seemed to always be rooting for Molly—even if it was a simple deadline to get some redlines in. But sitting in her late grandfather's living room and receiving a text from Lauren without one word asking how Molly's family was doing, seemed more aggravat-ing than knowing the competition was gaining speed.

Molly scrolled over their recent exchange. Huh. Not one condolence. Sure, Lauren had given Molly a heartfelt arm squeeze the day Molly found out about her grand-father's passing. That was something.

She skipped up to their last texting conversation, a couple weeks ago. Lauren had reached out saying she was sick and wouldn't be at work. Molly hardly acknowl-edged it in her response—just asked a question about work.

Wow.

Molly was more a stranger in her business relation-ship of nine hours a day—sometimes six days a week—for the past four years than she was in this home she hadn't stepped foot inside for a decade. Gran had picked up as if Molly had never left, as if she had served Molly breakfast, lunch and dinner every day of her twenty-eight years.

And Jack? He should have been all business too, es-pecially since the whole reason Molly extended her stay was to get this place ready to sell without a guarantee for his own livelihood. But he was so much more than business. He was kind, helpful and a daddy.

She crossed over and tucked the blanket a little closer to Tate's button chin. What was it with little motherless kids curling up on Gran's couch? Molly sighed and forced herself to stop thinking so much. She pulled out her to-do list and forced her heart to hibernate for a while.

By the time Molly had scheduled a walk-through via phone, taken some work calls and quietly decluttered the living room, she stood in the middle of the house, debating whether to risk completely wearing out her arms by painting trim or to opt for cleaning cobwebs out of the corners and leaving the oak trim for the next owner. Mainly, though, she kept glancing at the clock, wondering when Jack would join them. Every time she was caught off guard by the passing of time, her stomach twisted thinking that Jack would be here soon.

The breathing treatment seemed to do the trick when Tate woke up. Gran texted Jack around two and let him know all was well. A couple hours later, Jack showed up, hopefully ready to put on his handyman cap. His voice rumbled from the kitchen where Gran and Tate were clearing off the countertops and storing appliances in plastic totes—well, except the coffeepot. That was a must until the very last second in this old house.

Molly quickly reworked her ponytail. Out of habit, of course. She patted her pocket to find her lip gloss but then reprimanded herself.

No need. She did not need to freshen up for Jack. Old instincts, maybe. Although not one negative thought came to her mind about Jack, only rose-colored memories of her own first days of young love.

Every memory with Jack in it, anyway. She'd refused to go down memory lane by spending too much time focused on the one untouched corner of the room. Molly had worked on everything but the photo wall. Should it be up to her to dismantle the family-photo section?

"Wow, this place is bare," Jack exclaimed when he walked into the room. Every tabletop and shelf was wiped clean. Only a few vases with fake bouquets and pictures of generic landscapes were staged for pops of color.

"Yep. The real estate agent we met with today confirmed that we should make this place as impersonal as possible." Molly placed her hands on her hips and swiveled around, as if she was examining her work. But really, she tried to spin away the effect Jack had on her. He was as handsome as ever in this golden-lit room. She hardly recognized him as the guy she'd crushed on years ago. Now, he was this considerate friend, a man who had his share of heartache and seemed genuinely concerned for her own wounded heart.

"What about the wall?" Jack asked, stepping closer to Molly. He leaned a hand on the armchair between them.

Molly didn't follow his eyes but stood and faced him square on. She'd rather be uncomfortably trapped in his all-consuming gaze than scan the pictures of a time she'd long forgotten: that Easter when she was young enough to be held on Mom's hip; and those Christmas photos of her parents standing together beneath mistletoe on the porch. Molly didn't remember any such times of peace, and in not remembering, she grew more resentful toward the tumultuous past that stuck with her in the loneliest of moments.

"Think you might have some time to do the honors?" She slid her hands in her back pockets and cocked her head. She slipped back into her teen habit of allowing her ponytail to swoosh while flashing a coy smile. Yet, whatever discomfort she pushed away seemed to be attached to her lip. Wobbling and twitching and sending Jack the warning symbol that Molly Jansen was still a bit of a mess no matter how many years had passed.

"Of course I can do that." He sat on the arm of the chair, eye level with Molly now, and reached his hand across the chair's back. Molly imagined herself tucked against his chest with his arm securely around her. "I totally get it." He rubbed her elbow with that outstretched hand, and Molly didn't resist.

She leaned in and placed her hand on his arm. "Jack, you've been nothing but a friend since I've been here. I haven't had one of those in a really long time."

His dimples appeared, but his smile shone brightest in his rounded brown eyes. He placed his other hand on hers and squeezed. "Anytime, Mol."

The sound of the clock on the mantel was drowned out by the pulse in Molly's ears. She melted beneath his secure grasp. Finally shoving away the barricade around her senses she'd tried to maintain when Jack was around, her overly worked reasoning faded away. Slipping her hand from his, he tossed her a look of hurt—almost as if she was the one breaking hearts today—but she only trailed her hand down Jack's arm to lock her fingers with his. She didn't look at him, only their fingers twined together. With another squeeze from Jack, Molly's eyes darted up. She had forgotten his ability to embrace her with just a look. A warm, unpretentious, embracing gaze.

He shifted forward onto a knee in the chair, leaned over and cupped her cheek. "Molly, there really is one thing I wish that I could change."

"What is that?"

"That time might stand still so we can try this again."

"Try…this?" Molly's heart jerked about her chest knowing exactly what he meant. And suddenly all the skyscrapers in Chicago caught up with her in small-town Iowa, casting a dark shadow on the heart of this home where time threatened to race ahead. And for the first time since she'd arrived, she wished she could stay a good long while.

Jack leaned his forehead against hers, then gently pressed his lips to her own. Molly's eyes fluttered shut as she flooded with affection renewed just a few feet from the place of their very first kiss. She focused on these few seconds, pulsing with complete satisfaction that she had found home again. And while she tried with all her strength to push away the dwindling time here to the very corners of Austin Farm, her heart began to slow at a stark realization: there was no future here.

Jack was no longer managing his living in survival mode like he thought. Holding Molly close, kissing her as if they had no time left—which they hardly did, with her big life in Chicago only days away—whatever the truth about all this was, Jack hadn't felt this alive in such a long time. He didn't want this to end too quickly. Her lips were soft and sweet. The exhilaration bursting in his chest obliterated the struggle to just get to the next day without a trip to urgent care or the unemployment office. Right here, right now, was a sudden electric bolt of assurance that life could be good again.

When a cell ringtone pierced the air, Molly groaned against his lips and pulled away. "I better check that." Her cheeks were bright red. Whatever Jack felt inside his chest was radiating in her beautiful eyes. Expectant, bright, ecstatic. She rested her teeth on her lip, and her lashes covered her blues in a quick curtsy, then she leaned in and grazed his lips again before pulling completely away and rushing to the desk to grab her phone.

Jack crumpled into the armchair and ran his fingers through his hair, feeling like winter was upon him with all Molly's warmth just a few feet away.

"Really? You heard him say that?" Molly swiveled around. She was radiant, with a lopsided smile and her hand cupping her face. "Thanks, Lauren. I will definitely send over my conceptuals. I can't wait to get back and chat with him face to face." She tucked her chin down into her chest, said *uh-huh* and *sounds good* a few more times, then said, "Bye for now" and ended the call. She cradled the phone in both hands and held it to her chest.

"Well?" Jack rose against a tidal wave of reality. "Looks like you got some good news."

She nodded quickly. Dark strands of hair dislodged from her ponytail and brushed along her nose. Molly swiped them away, tucking them behind her ear. "Just the senior partner saying that he is *most* interested in my concept—as he remembers my contribution to our last team collaboration." She squealed. "Honestly, I just brainstormed—didn't even get to work on the project. But I guess I did have the initial idea that was eventually implemented in the final presentation to the client." She jumped up on her toes. "I cannot believe he remembered that! And he even booked the conference room for a consult with me next week."

Jack chuckled and drew close. "That's great, Molly. You are pretty unforgettable."

She tilted her head in the cutest way possible, looking up at him with one eye closed, as if he was a hundred feet above her. Although it was not even a foot, Jack could be up in the clouds right now if he wasn't such a realist. If he could just live in this moment, without allowing the very true fact that Molly was not here to stay. And her phone call confirmed their brief second had certainly passed and the kisses were more foolish than life-giving. He took a step back. Molly's lips parted, then she stepped back too.

"So." He rocked on his heels and turned toward the photo wall. "I'll get started on this wall for you…"

Molly placed her hand on his arm. She stood beside him, staring at the wall. "Jack, I… I don't know what else to do."

Against the energy running through his veins, the desire to turn around and scoop her up and promise her life here would be spectacular if she'd consider trying to renew something he'd cut off so quickly—an obviously irrational thought—he dipped his chin to find her blue eyes wide with surrender. "This wall, and that newel and the creaky stair. Those are our tasks right now."

"But…" her gaze boomeranged to the armchair then up to him again "…us? What about us?"

Jack gritted his teeth, knowing he should end this before it really began, but staring at the girl who first stole part of his heart long ago and now revived his whole heart into a swelling drum. "Aren't you the one who likes to dream up fantastical plans?" He snickered, swallowing back bile. "I'm thinking we just had a weak moment of fantasy." He winked. "Don't worry. You have so much more to look forward to…" *Than Jack Behrens…than this life of struggling to make ends meet…than desperately striving to stay on top of meds and doctor's vis-*

its for a medically fragile superhero. "You are living a dream, Mol. Don't let this simple farmer stop you."

Her shoulders drooped, and she pushed her chin up and frowned. "Simple? C'mon, Jack. You are far from that." She lifted on her tiptoes and kissed his cheek. "Time caught up with us, I guess." She lowered and crammed her hands in her jean pockets. "Better get going. We have a walk through with an agent at four."

Jack filled his lungs and strode over to the first picture. Rob and Gertie's photo from the church directory. He stared hard at the man with the wise eyes, steady, assured smile, and who'd secured Jack's future while he lived and breathed.

"Hey, Jack," Molly called out.

"Yeah?"

"The real estate agent said she is going to include your credentials too. Hopefully everything will work out for all of us."

Jack faced her and gave a curt nod. "I really appreciate that. Hope so."

But the lump in his throat signaled that hope might be part of the fantasy and it was time to wake up. He had to come to the conclusion that Molly's leaving was sabotaging his focus on the practical. How could a week with an ex-girlfriend mess with his priorities at this stage in the game?

As he began to take down pictures of life lived long ago, he tried to focus on all that was needed now. But a gnawing suspicion hinted that it would be near impossible to imagine that life would ever be the same after kissing Molly Jansen.

Chapter Sixteen

When Jack and Tate left later that afternoon, Molly tried to scrape away all her disappointment with the wallpaper in Gran's bathroom. Kissing Jack was the last thing on her to-do list and a fantasy that she had left on the porch the night he broke up with her.

She chipped away at a particularly stubborn clump of old glue. Was she being honest with herself? Not really. Her flutters had been at full force in the garage this morning. And just before Jack walked in this afternoon, she had to force herself to leave her lip gloss in her pocket.

Yeah, Molly was not too disappointed in that kiss. In fact, her old knack for fantasy hopped from the sensation of his sweet lips on hers to dreaming up long-distance phone calls and racing across that Mississippi for future weekend kisses too. Her mind was an Olympic athlete when it came to racing well ahead of her current situation.

The weekend flew by in Molly's world of design but dragged on without Tate and Jack around. Jack had told Gran there were a couple of baseball playoff games, and he had to catch up on things at home. But Molly wondered if practicing space was a wise move on Jack's part.

While she got ready on Monday, her nerves frenzied as if it were Christmas morning. But as she passed the front window, Jack's truck pulled out and turned up the side road to the metal building where the machinery was stored. She chided her deflated heart for missing him.

Tate pedaled into the living room on the old John Deere toy tractor.

"Hey, Miss Molly. Want to get in the cart, and I'll take us to get some ice cream?"

Molly spied the cart attached to the back of the tractor. She planted her hands on her hips and feigned a look of bewilderment. "Tate, my foot wouldn't even fit in that."

He covered his giggles with his hand. "I know. I'm just teasing." He coughed in his elbow. "What are you doing today?" Tate pedaled around the couch. *Squeak, click. Squeak, click.*

"Going to tidy up the mudroom." She peeked out the window above the old air-conditioning unit. Jack's truck was out of sight.

"I'll help you!" Tate dismounted his toy, caught up to her, let out a big breath and clutched her hand. Small fingers clinging to hers. A new sensation for Molly. So sweet. Yet so…temporary. How could she even consider complicating Jack's life with a long-distance relationship? She rolled her eyes. How foolish. How selfish, really. She didn't need Jack's attention, this little guy did. She couldn't scoot into his life and upend things.

Molly had the scars of a child whose parent's love life shoved Molly aside, time and again. To expect Jack to continue managing his own career, his amazing son and a long-distance relationship? No, no, no. She pushed open the mudroom door, releasing all the heart-shaped butterflies from her tummy, and asking God to help keep her goal clear and her heart at a steady, unaffected pace. No Olympic-speed vitals, no excitable thoughts, no hopeful interactions with Jack.

They started on the closet, pushing back the bifold doors. Shelves were full of half-used detergent bottles, gardening tools, towels and anything that had found its way into the house but never made it past the kitchen.

"What's this?" Tate was on his knees pulling out a pink plastic box.

Molly gasped. "Oh, Tate!" She grabbed it from him and sat down cross-legged. "These are my Lego. Do you have some?"

Tate nodded. His breathing was visible. Shoulders up, down, and his shirt crinkled at his chest. A high-pitched wheeze was just detectible.

Molly brushed her fingers through his hair across his forehead. "You okay, bud? Should we get your dad?"

He shook his head. "No, Miss Molly. I want to see." He raised his eyebrows with impatience and ogled the box.

Molly lifted the lid. A half-finished creation sat on top of hundreds of Lego pieces. Memories slammed into her mind, and she lifted the piece created with only yellow bricks. "If I remember correctly, this was going to be a special room."

Tate jerked his head back. "A room? That doesn't look like a room."

She smiled. "Well, it was going to have four walls. See? I only got to two."

"What happened?" Tate took the *L*-shaped creation and studied it. "Why didn't you finish?"

Molly cast her eyes to the ceiling, noting the cobwebs with great attention. How could she be thankful for cobwebs? Maybe because she didn't really want to search for the answer to Tate's question. But it struck her with great force. Mom had arrived that day she sat here with the Lego bin to pack up her things. Her things, not her daughter. And that was not the last time she left. Would take a few more years. Smack dab in the middle of Molly's senior year.

She cleared her throat and answered, "I grew up."

"I have lots of unfinished buildings too. Mommy got too sick to help me." Tate's forehead was furrowed as he dug through the colorful bricks and fished out yellow ones. "I ask Dad to help me finish them, but he's always too busy." His tone was matter-of-fact. He wore only determination on his face. Not an ounce of remorse, sadness or grief. He just kept digging through the Lego, taking it upon himself to collect the rest of the pieces for Molly's childhood build. Swallowing hard past a growing lump in her throat, she watched Tate living on without his mom at the tender age of four, while she couldn't get over the loss of her own mother at twenty-eight.

The sound of the back door opening and closing signaled that Gran was probably going to the garden like she'd mentioned over coffee early this morning. But Jack appeared at the mudroom doorway. He gave a nod of acknowledgment to her but cast his gaze on Tate whose back was to him.

Tate exclaimed, "Hey! I have an idea. If I help you finish yours, will you come help me finish mine?" His freckles danced about his cheeks as the widest smile grew beneath sky-blue eyes.

Before Molly answered, Jack said, "I think Miss Molly has real buildings to finish, Tater." He leaned against the doorjamb, keeping his eyes on his son. "I forgot his nebulizer at my house. Just making sure everything's going okay before I head home again."

Molly stood. "Yeah. Maybe check him. He seems to be laboring a bit."

"Thanks," Jack said and gave a tight smile. Molly took a step back and focused on the little boy.

He was staring up at her. "Miss Molly, if I help you get all the chores done here, you can help me at my house."

Molly cast an uneasy look at Jack. He opened his mouth to speak, but Molly blurted, "You know, Tate, I have a lot of work to do besides the chores. How about you bring over your favorite tomorrow and work on it here?"

"Oh, not sure if he's coming here tomorrow." Jack squatted next to Tate and tucked his finger under Tate's chin, examining his face. "I don't like the sound of that breathing. Your lips are a little blue."

"I don't want Aunt Lisa to watch me. I want to stay here." Tate pulled his face away and continued with the Lego.

"Sorry, bud. That's the plan." Jack stood. He glanced at Molly. "We'll head home and get that breathing treatment, then I will bring him back. Tell Gertie I'll grab those old chairs she wanted to get rid of when we return."

Molly was still processing the fact that this was Tate's last day here. She just stared at him, wondering if she would see him again. "You think you will still bring Tate over after work?" Her words sounded garbled. Molly couldn't disqualify her heart from the race. It refused to stay slow and steady.

A small crinkle appeared between Jack's eyebrows. His nostrils flared, and he spoke in a low tone, "Maybe. I am not sure what tomorrow holds." He grimaced and dropped his gaze to the floor tile. "When do you plan to leave?"

Suddenly she felt like a cheating contestant who didn't deserve a medal. "Hoping to leave Friday. Could use the weekend to scout out my project's property in case I am missing anything before I chat with the senior partner the following Monday."

Jack responded with long, heavy nods.

Tate scrambled to his feet. "You'll be back, right?" He gathered her hand in his again. Jack cupped Tate's shoulder. Molly forced a smile and squeezed his little fingers. "Of course. Gran will need help moving."

"Good. And maybe you can help me then." Tate began to cough into his arm.

"C'mon, son. Let's figure out what we need to do to get you back in superhero mode." Jack lifted Tate up, and he laid his head on Jack's shoulder. "Sometimes, kids keep on going even when they feel crummy," he explained to Molly as he turned into the kitchen. "And Tate has a huge tolerance for feeling crummy when Lego is involved." He chuckled. "Guess I owe him some building time."

Molly followed them and held open the back door as they passed through. Maybe that sentiment of owing time was a typical dad one. She had always hoped for more time with her own dad, but he couldn't manage much, working two jobs just to pay off old debt.

Jack continued down the back porch to his truck, while Tate snuggled closer to his father's neck.

Molly's heart ached and warmed all at once. Her own father had once held her like that. There was such security in that small space etched out from a dad's jaw, his neck and his shoulder. One of her favorite things to do as a child was tuck her face in that exact spot, inhale Dad's spicy-scented aftershave and warm up her whole face with her breathing during a typical Iowa winter day. She had been blessed with a good daddy. Even if he couldn't give her the time she probably could have used.

Jack cast a sorrowful look at her over the truck door. Relentless aching outmatched her sweet memories. The discomfort radiated and overwhelmed every other thought. She was not a child feeling bad, but easily distracted.

She was completely consumed by feeling crummy.

Her ache was long and wide and deep.

And resisting running down the steps to soak up whatever minutes were left, she stepped away, blaming her misery on this impulsive notion of a second chance at love with Jack Behrens.

After Tate's breathing treatment at home, Jack dropped him off again on his way to meet up with Wade Grover. Even though he and Tate had kept busy this weekend, his mind was sluggish, begging to return to that living room where time stopped—albeit briefly so.

That afternoon, Jack took on painting the porch while Molly and Gran worked inside. He wasn't thrilled about the self-assigned isolation, but he knew it was the wise choice.

The next morning, Lisa suggested she wait one more

day to expose Tate to her family, so Jack set up Tate with his breathing treatment at Gertie's. Gertie held up the white paper bag from the pharmacy as Jack plugged in the nebulizer by the armchair. "That's the last of the albuterol. Better call in a refill, Jack."

"Will do." He carefully placed the elastic band of the mask over Tate's head, making a mental note to put a reminder in his phone. "Okay, bud. Deep breaths." He flipped the machine on. The plastic mask began to fog with the cloudy mist. Jack prayed that the medicine would work fast and effectively.

He stood and pulled out his phone and typed in *Call pharmacy at 8 am*. Brittany would have noted all the meds that needed a refill and called them in at once. Jack chided himself for his multiple trips to the drug store.

He spied Molly from his peripheral and tried to just focus on his Reminders app. But she was hauling a chair that he was supposed to bring down.

"Let me get that," he offered, crossing the room to meet her at the front door.

"It's okay, I can manage." Her tone was reminiscent of her first day back.

"Oh, yes, city girl, I know you can." He raised an eyebrow with all the snark he could muster.

"Back to that, are we?" She rolled her eyes, then tossed a compassionate glance to Tate. "How's he doing?"

Jack opened the door for her and followed her to the porch. She set the chair down next to the newly repaired post, then spun around.

Jack leaned on the wall beside the door. All the weird tension between them was left behind the screen door that lagged and clicked closed. Right now, his anxiety heightened as Molly's blue eyes rounded with concern.

"The meds should help. It's hard to not consider what's going on inside him." He stared past her toward the old grain bin across the road. "All I keep thinking is how his lungs are just filling up, drowning him. Like he's stuck in a grain bin with a whole harvest of corn dumping on top of him."

"Should he go to the doctor?"

"He has his quarterly CF checkup on Thursday. Hoping we can avoid an urgent care visit till then."

"Maybe if you took him, you'd have some peace until his checkup."

"And risk him picking up all those germs in a sick waiting room?" He hooked his hand behind his neck. "It's a risk I don't want to take if I don't have to. Hoping to just stay on top of treatment until the doctor can look at his lungs."

"That's a hard call to make, Jack. It sounds complicated." Her words were gentle with compassion. "He's a blessed kid to have a dad like you."

He narrowed his eyes, trying to push away the temptation of allowing her kindness to slice through the boundary of distance needed—physically between them on this porch, and inevitably at the end of the week.

Molly's jaw flinched. "I really do mean it." She turned away and snatched up the chair again.

"I know you do, Mol. Sorry, I am just struggling with everything."

She looked over her shoulder so he could just make out her profile. In a high-pitched tone she said, "Me too." Her lashes hovered over her cheeks as she stared down at the space between them. "I am so proud of you, Jack.

You've made me realize that I have focused so much on my mom's failings, I don't give my dad much credit. But he was a good one too. You keep up loving that sweet boy. He'll be so thankful one day."

She opened her mouth as if to speak again but, instead, continued down the steps. He followed her around the house to the burn pile.

The corn was at its greenest. Soon, all the leaves would begin to dry. The emerald green would fade to gold, and harvest would come. Most of Jack's work these days was preparing for harvest. Fixing machinery, emptying the grain bins, meeting with John Deere reps. Everything culminated at harvest. He loved the journey. The anticipation.

He stood on the opposite side of the burn pile from Molly. They usually lit it right around harvest. But this year would be different since Gertie's move was fast approaching.

Molly tossed the chair with a broken arm on top of the old porch post. "I don't even remember that chair," she said and sniffled. "But I saw the name on the bottom." She grimaced. "Mom's."

"Oh, I'm sorry, Molly."

Molly shrugged and spun around, walked between two stalks, then peered up at each on either side of her. The corn was about Jack's height, looming above Molly's petite frame.

"Looks like it's a good crop this year." She tucked her hands in her back pockets, her arms bent in such a way that he could easily slip both arms around her waist and pull her close. What was wrong with him? She's talking farming, and he's standing here daydreaming.

He sighed and strode over to her. "Yep, we've had

just the right amount of rain and heat. Been a beautiful summer."

"Guess this is a bittersweet kind of summer." She took another step into the row. "Grandad's passing, my project…unfinished Lego creations, sweet Tate…you…" Her shoulders sagged, then began to shake. "How could she?" Her words mingled with sobs behind her hand. She spun around and Jack stepped in, wrapping his arms around her as if he had practiced for this his whole life. She shuddered against him, and he pulled her closer. Her apple-scented shampoo rose amid the earthy aroma of farmland. He pressed his cheek gently upon her head and squeezed his eyes shut. She mumbled, "I… I am sorry. At every turn, I am faced with Mom. I wish that I could feel peace with how everything turned out for me—for her. But how can anyone find peace with where she ended up?" Her arms wrapped around his torso, and she squeezed closer.

"I am so sorry, Mol. I know that Brittany is in a good place, and peace is still hard to come by."

She tilted her head up. Her lashes were dark with moisture, and remnants of freckles dusted her nose. "You've been through so much. I probably need to grow up." She looked down again.

"Don't say that. We all have our trials. And when there's no closure…it's downright difficult."

She laughed against his chest. "When did you get to be so smart?"

When did you get to be so irresistible? He clamped his mouth shut. *No, do not go there again.* She was heading directly east in a few days. His nostrils flared. But what about today? This chance to just be together again, for just a little while?

A sudden wave of excitement gripped him at the thought of this moment. This chance—today. To just be with Molly Jansen while she was here with him.

"Hey, I have an idea." Jack pulled back and locked his fingers with hers.

"What?"

"Let's go." He began to walk deeper into the field, the sharp edges of leaves stinging his arms, but he didn't care.

"Where?"

"To stake out that room you want to build."

Molly guffawed. "Jack, c'mon. That's ridiculous."

"If I build one…" he swiveled on his heel and with all the authenticity he could muster said, "…will you come back?"

She stepped back. "What?"

Jack would work the rest of his life without land to farm if he might have a chance at facing Molly's vibrancy day in and day out. She brought him to life again. "What if we can make this work? I was so practical when you talked about heading back. I mean, you are this amazing architect on the brink of a promotion. And I am a dad and farmer attached to this land. There is no way a long-distance relationship crossed my mind." Jack stepped closer and cradled her hands against his chest. "Until now. Until I realized how much we fit together, Molly. I wasn't grown-up enough back then to be all you needed. But I am here now, and I am pretty grown-up. More than I ever wanted to be. And you are beautiful. So beautiful. From the inside out. My kid adores you. I adore you."

"Oh, Jack. We've switched places." She wagged her head and exhaled. "You are dreaming. I want so badly to dream right along with you. But I just can't. I may have backslid into fantasy this week, but I've grown up…and away. Nowhere in my future is settling down in farm country. Making it work for a while makes little sense if I know that my home will never be in the same zip code as yours. Besides, it wouldn't be fair to you or Tate. You all will never have all of me."

"Ouch. When you put it that way, it stings. Not going to lie."

"I am sorry. I don't mean to be harsh, but it's true."

He had held back on giving her his full attention back in high school. And she'd got burned in the end. Molly knew what it was like to not have all of someone. If only her words tamed the wild stampede inside him, but they didn't. He only wanted her more.

The blinds shot up from the living room on the other side of the burn pile. Jack released Molly's hands and stepped back.

"Let's go check on Tate." He strode past her, tempted to snag her hand on the way. But his little boy was the only priority now, and Molly admitted her allegiance was hundreds of miles away. The possibility of making this work seemed as silly as digging out a room in the center of a cornfield. Building it would be tricky, and its fate was inevitable. It wouldn't last. The whole field was destined to be torn down in the end.

Chapter Seventeen

The next day, Molly plodded down the stairs of a strangely quiet house, her heart sore from that last conversation with Jack. She followed the quiet clinking of dishes into the kitchen. Gran was stirring oatmeal on the stovetop.

"So strange not having cartoons cranked up over that machine of Tate's," Molly said as she wrapped her arm around Gran's shoulder with a good-morning squeeze.

"I am glad I'm not moving too far away. Jack promises to visit me," Gran replied, knocking the spoon on the edge of the pot. "Hopefully your great recommendation to the agent yesterday will help keep him on this land." She offered a coy smile in Molly's direction. "You appreciate him, don't you?" The fine lines around her mouth grew deeper, and her eyes flashed as she walked over and poured oatmeal into two bowls.

Heat crept up Molly's neck as she lowered into her seat. Just talking about Jack swarmed her senses with anticipation. When would she catch his sparkling gaze next? Could she manage to keep her heart at a distance now that it was fully awake and longing for the boy-turned-handsome-farmer of her dreams?

"Gran, you know that everything I said was true." Molly played aloof well. She'd had six years in a cut-throat design firm to practice. "Besides, Jack has been a great friend to me. I should at least try to help him."

"Friend?" Gran smirked and offered her a spoon. "You all looked like a whole lot more than friends outside yesterday."

"Gran!"

"Well, I couldn't help but wonder what took so long to take that chair out to the burn pile. And I accidently spied you all holding hands." She sat down across from her. "Oh, sweet girl, I can't help but wonder what a good pair you two would make."

Molly lunged her chair back and stood. "Out of the question. I am so close to making my own dream come true, and Jack has plenty to do without me occasionally distracting him." She set her untouched bowl in the sink then spun around, wrapping her arms across her chest to give off the impression of a closed discussion. But her stance was most needed to contain the wild storm within her. "Please, Gran, let's drop it—"

Her phone rang from the other room.

As she hurried from the kitchen, Gran called, "Saved by the bell, honey. But you still have time for a change of heart." Her jolly chuckle, while at Molly's expense, did warm the place. Gran was in a good mood, and Molly hoped she would continue to have good spirits through the rest of this transition.

Molly's office number popped up on her cell-phone screen. "Hello, this is Molly."

"Molly! You will never believe this." Lauren's voice

screeched through the phone. "They bumped up presentations to Friday. Are you going to be ready on Friday?"

"What?" Whatever flush had overtaken Molly during her talk with Gran was replaced with panic freezing her very breath to lodge itself in her throat. "There…there is no way I am ready to present on Friday. I wanted to meet with the partner first."

"Something about needing to bump up timelines because of the client's schedule." Lauren sounded like she was pacing. The distant ding of an elevator arose in the background. She must be in the lobby to stay clear of prying ears. "Anyway, they were all huddled around Harleson's desk…and I'll just say this, it wasn't a nonchalant chat."

Molly groaned and frantically woke her computer with a firm tap on the power button. "I have too much to do. I mean, I can't leave yet. I told the real estate agent we would have the house ready to go on the market this weekend. I am in the middle of painting a bathroom…and the hardware hasn't been replaced… I am not ready—"

"Molly. This is something you've been working toward your whole career. Are you telling me you are going to give it up?" Lauren's words were sharp and slicing.

Molly shook her head and managed to say, "No, of course not. I will get it done. I will get it all done." She ended the call and crumpled into the desk chair, raking her hands through her hair.

"What's the matter, dear?" Gran stood over her shoulder.

"I just… I need to go back to Chicago to get this project done. Sooner than later." Molly swiveled in the seat and cast a pleading look to Gran. "Do you think you can manage getting the rest ready? I mean, I will be back in a week…or two."

If Gran had a couple more seconds to process what Molly was asking, Molly assumed she would easily brush away any worry and assure her that she could leave. But between her happy countenance in the kitchen and Molly's self-serving request, Gran only appeared completely astonished. "I planned to move before Labor Day… I-I need to get this place sold."

Molly couldn't stand upsetting Gran. She straightened in her chair and waved a hand. "Don't listen to me." She forced a smile. "That was a momentary lapse of sanity. It's all good."

"Are you sure—"

Molly hopped out of the chair and began to head upstairs. "If I can get that bathroom finished, then I'll spend some time on my project. And Jack's coming this afternoon, right?"

"I believe so."

"Great. We make a good team. I am sure we can get this all finished up—and I can get my project squared away." She turned up the stairs and flashed Gran a smile across the living room. "Don't worry. It's all good, Gran. We will be ready before Friday."

And Molly was going to hopefully hit the road before then. She needed to swing by the client's property and get her bearings to make sure her concept wasn't completely fantastical. It seemed she'd been living in a whole lot of fantasy these days.

It was time for Molly Jansen to resume her practical, focused architect mindset. She had worked too hard to let this opportunity pass her by because she was stuck in Polk Center with a chores list and a farmer. Albeit a cute one.

Jack got off the phone with Tate's doctor just as Lisa arrived with little Elise on her hip. The screen door closed behind them, and she set Elise down. The toddler immediately climbed up the steps on her knees, and Jack swooped her up and spun her around.

"I've missed you, pumpkin." The squeals and giggles of his only niece coaxed some joy. Not enough to flip his frown, though.

"You look tired," Lisa said as she joined them in the living room.

Jack put Elise down, and she toddled down the hallway toward Tate's room. "I had hoped that he would be at his healthiest for his quarterly appointment." Lisa rubbed his shoulder, then took her diaper bag to the console table outside the bathroom. "Doc called in some more meds. Going to pick them up this afternoon."

Jack's phone chimed. He checked it. An email from the seed company.

"Here we go," he muttered.

"What's that?" Lisa headed to the kitchen and began to fill the kettle.

Jack rolled his neck, then straddled a bar stool at the counter opposite his sister. "Got an interview to work at the seed company."

Lisa's jaw dropped. "Are you kidding? I thought that's the last thing you wanted—an office job."

"I need to stay around here, Lees. Can't imagine doing this without you all nearby."

Lisa turned the burner on, then crossed over and

placed her hand on top of his. "I am sorry about Austin Farm. Seemed like a refuge for you."

"Still is, I guess." Jack clenched his jaw. With Molly around, it seemed like so much more than a refuge, though. "You remember Molly, don't you?"

Lisa shifted her eyes up to the ceiling, then pursed her lips. "Uh…yeah. That year you dated was the same year I started high school. Talk about drama."

Jack grimaced. "She was going through a hard time back then."

Lisa shook her head. "No, I was talking about you. You seemed awestruck by her but always suckered into some social event or a school-pride extravaganza." Her shoulders lifted with a chuckle. "You didn't know who you should be—debonair boyfriend or Mr. Popular Quarterback."

"Wow, you remember it like that?"

"Trust me, I had all these girls talking to me about my senior brother, but then I saw you with Molly…and knew that you were pretty much taken." She smiled. "I presume the rumors are true. She's a stunning architect now?"

Jack nodded and swallowed hard. "*Stunning* is an understatement." He began to laugh. "She's something else, Lees. Wish all of Polk Center could see her now. She's so driven. Following her dream…and somehow, she's captured Tate's heart too—" Jack clamped his mouth a tad too late. His whole face heated up.

Lisa's eyes flashed with intrigue. "I haven't seen that look in a long time…" Her whole face softened. "You seem happy, Jack." Lisa dipped her chin and raised her eyebrows in a give-me-details kind of look.

Jack just lowered his attention to the email waiting for his response. "Doesn't matter. She's not staying here."

Lisa folded her arms across her torso. "Wow, big brother, I didn't expect repairing an old farmhouse would become grounds for fixing up an old relationship."

He shook his head. "Nope, there's no fixing up involved. Her heart's in Chicago, and mine is just down the hall."

"Nothing's impossible, Jack," Lisa rolled her eyes. "I wouldn't be surprised if God has something in the works. You deserve some happiness."

"I will be plenty happy if Tate's appointment goes well." Jack leaned back in his stool. Although, his heart thrummed double speed with all this talk about Molly.

"Of course. We all will be happy for that." Lisa squeezed his arm. "God works all things for our good, remember? You finding love again is a good thing."

"I didn't say anything about love," Jack blurted.

"Oh sure, that's true." Lisa turned to the whistling kettle. "Just remember God's got this…" She removed the kettle off the burner and began to fix a cup of tea.

There were no more words to say. Jack was cornered between his heart and his faith. Seemed like they should be the same thing, but fear gripped him at the thought that all this time he was doubting God, God was still working on his behalf, anyway. This email for an interview was proof. His little boy's health up to this point was a blessing. And Molly? Well, he just couldn't go there right now. No matter what Lisa suggested. If he was supposed to be with Molly, Jack had to trust God to make it happen. There really was nothing Jack could do but pray.

Chapter Eighteen

Molly had never painted a room as quickly as she slathered the bathroom walls with soft gray to erase the baby pink of the sixties. After lugging the rest of the paint downstairs and setting it outside Gran's bathroom door, she gathered up her things and decided she needed all the vibes of Grandad's creative space to get her project up to presentation level.

"I'll be in the garage, Gran," she called over her shoulder and heard a muffled acknowledgment from the closet under the stairs.

She snagged one of Gran's famous Stroopwafels from a plate on the counter and headed outside. The air was hot and sticky, and the day was as bright as ever. Could she concentrate on her work in this heat? Molly surprised herself with doubt. Nothing ever stopped Molly Jansen from working before. Why would she be concerned now?

She used her elbow to turn the handle of the garage door, set her stuff on the workbench and turned on the standing fan. She didn't have time to consider if the air was cool enough. She set to work right away, munching on the sweet caramel sandwich of waffle cookies.

Every section of her project sparked some memory of her past days with Tate, Gran and, mostly, Jack. Certain elements of her past designs would bring to mind whatever podcast or movie she had listened to or watched as she worked, but this time, she'd worked in the pockets between sweet exchanges with a special little boy and flirtations with an old sweetheart. Her project was the background noise to some pretty fabulous moments.

She glanced out the window to see if she'd catch a glimpse of Jack. Nope, not anywhere in view. Probably a very good thing.

After working for an hour, something was off. She studied the original topography map and realized she had missed a key element of the land, destroying whatever fluidity she hoped to achieve in the structure. The focal point of the most picturesque window in the place was obstructed.

She tossed her pencil down and shoved away from the workbench.

The door opened, and Gran appeared. "How's it going?"

"Not great," Molly grumbled. "I made a huge mistake."

Gran crossed over and set two lunch sacks on the workbench. "I am sure you will fix it, dear. Nothing has ever stopped you before."

Agitated, Molly stood and crossed her arms. "You really can't understand." Her throat burned with agitation. "I was foolish to think I could put my life on hold. I feel like everything is just slipping away."

Gran opened her mouth to speak but didn't say anything.

"I need a break," Molly said under her breath and

started to the door. "It's so hot and sticky, I think my brain is turning to mush."

"That's a good idea," Gran exclaimed. "Why don't you take some lunch down to Jack?"

Molly swiveled and gaped at her. "How will that help?"

"You said you needed a break." Gran stepped forward and handed both sacks to her. "Nobody's at their best on an empty stomach, farmer and architect alike."

Molly reluctantly took the lunches.

"Jack said he would be working on the equipment today. At the old metal building." She smiled. "Mol, you are great no matter what happens with your project. You know that, right?"

"Gran," she said, exasperated. Gran had talked to her the same way when Molly crammed for finals her junior year.

"Well, it's true. Your dream is only important because it's yours. But it doesn't make you better or worse. It is just something you desire, not something that defines you."

"See? I don't think you do understand." Molly let out a sour laugh. "It's really all I have. My work."

"What about me?" Gertie scoffed, a flicker of hurt in her eyes.

"Of course I have you. But day in and day out, my work is it. You aren't in Chicago."

"And you aren't just *you* in Chicago. You have folks here that love you. You have a life that's yours—right here." Gran cupped Molly's cheek and kissed her forehead.

Molly inhaled a shaky breath, trying to support the protest forming on her lips. A few days ago, she would have corrected Gran and said there was only one soul keeping her connected to this place. But that was before Jack filled up her view, distracted her working time with sweet conversation and introduced her to the fantastic Tate.

She had folks here. And she tried her best to resist thinking deeper than knowing them—even though loving them seemed so much more life-giving than the project on her screen.

Molly held up the lunch sacks and said, "Thanks," then headed out the garage and down the path to the far side of the property. Gran's garden was lush on the left, and the corn was tall on the right. Her boat shoes crunched the gravel on the narrow drive to the back side of the steel building where the farm equipment was stored. The garage doors were up, and the machines were exactly how she remembered them. Green with yellow accents, cold engines and filling up the space with all the anticipation of an abundant yield.

Jack approached between two tractors, wiping his hands on an old rag. "Hey, there. You are a sight for sore eyes."

Molly rolled her eyes. "Clichés?"

Jack laughed and shook his head. "Sorry, but haven't had a great morning. Just calling 'em like I see 'em."

"Hmm, cliché number two." She smirked and held up a sack. "Gran made you lunch."

"And you too." He glanced at her other hand. "You going to eat with me?"

"Sure." She managed a smile without any snark or resistance. She'd never say it, but just seeing Jack settled her anxiety, taking the sore away from her eyes too.

His phone chimed. He pulled it out. "Oh, Tate's prescription is ready. Want to take lunch to go and come say hey to Tate?"

"Uh…" She glanced over her shoulder. "I have a lot of work to do…" But she really didn't want to think about all the work she had to do. So much redoing. Maybe a change of scenery would do her some good. "Sure, let's go. I was afraid I wouldn't see Tate again. Glad to surprise him."

Jack tossed the rag into a bucket and fished his keys out of his pocket. "He'll be happy. But he might try and get you to stay. Just warning you." He flashed a smile that activated those amazing dimples.

Molly's phone pinged, and she checked it. Lauren was following up. She turned the phone on Silent and followed Jack to his truck.

Jack tried to press into his faith that God would make this all work out. But Molly sitting in his truck, her hair loose and brushing against her shoulders, with a backdrop of sun-kissed cornfields out the window, revved up those high-school affections into grown-up longing.

She glanced over at him, and he focused on the road. "How is Tate doing?"

"He's okay. Still struggling, but this prescription will help. Thankful we've only got a day till he goes in for his checkup."

"How do they assess his lungs?"

"A PFT…pulmonary function test. Tate blows into a machine, and they check various measurements. I was hopeful he'd have a clean bill this time. Finally feels like we've figured out a good rhythm." His usual insecurity jostled his nerves, and he added, "Well, except that I haven't managed to play offense with the prescription refills. Constantly feeling behind on that."

"It's so much, Jack." Molly clutched at the paper sack in her lap. "I am beginning to understand how easy it is to drop a ball or two."

"You are?" Jack slid a gaze at her, noting her serious tone. "Did something happen with Gertie?"

"Oh no. I just got more carried away with..." she shifted in her seat and then turned to the window "...with fixing up the house. Missed an important detail on my project. I don't know that I was ever very good at multitasking." She sulked against the seat.

"Aw, I am sorry, Molly." Jack reached his hand between them, then paused, laying it on the seat close to his thigh. "Is it an easy fix?"

She shrugged her shoulders. "Just more grunt work to get to the good stuff, as Grandad would say." She cast a knowing smile in his direction. "I just feel like a mountain cropped up, though."

"Then, you just keep chipping away the rough to find that diamond."

Molly turned to him. Her smile bright and her eyes brighter. "You sound like an artist, Jack Behrens."

"Well, Rob offered me that analogy too." Molly's smile faded, and she just stared at him. He kept his eye on the road but sensed her gaze didn't waver. "When I was at my lowest, he told me that the hard stuff was necessary to find the treasure." His nostrils flared as he thought about Rob and Brittany and he swelled with grief. "I am hoping that I can continue to help Tate get through the hard stuff and that he will get a chance to find treasure of his own."

Molly's hand covered his. He looked over at her. Her

face shone with genuine affection. "You are an amazing person. I think Tate's treasure is you."

He swallowed hard, his Adam's apple knocking the collar of his T-shirt. "We've had hard stuff too, you and me. Think we are past it?" He turned his hand over and threaded their fingers together.

"High school? Yes, absolutely…"

"But…"

"When I go back?" Molly leaned her head back on the seat and turned to the window again. "The hardest thing is going to be saying goodbye."

You don't have to say goodbye, Jack wanted to say. But he had to stick to his word—his faith. Besides, Molly had just admitted that her time here had caused a mistake on the project of her life. He needed to respect her decision to focus on her career. "I think right now is the treasure. For me, anyway." He squeezed her hand, then pulled his away. "This last week with Molly Jansen. I won't forget it."

Chapter Nineteen

After they picked up the prescription, they drove past the town square. Molly had never considered how quaint this place was. She had changed, though. This unexpected reunion with Jack filtered some of the insecurity that seemed to have festered through the years. She watched him as they turned away from the center of Polk Center. His chiseled jawline was dusted with a five-o'clock shadow, and his lashes were long and dark. If he only knew how much his affirmations had convinced Molly she was bigger than her past. Molly had no ties to the assumptions of the town and the failings of her mom. Jack had only made her feel like a diamond from the rough. Although, the rough was years ago when everyone was young, not fully grown. Why was she so fearful of it coming to the surface upon her return?

Gran had reminded her that she was the same here as she was in Chicago. And it wasn't an insult. Gran spoke it to remind Molly how valued she was in both places.

Her chest constricted. That's what it was, wasn't it? Just like her project, she chipped away anything that would connect her to the girl of her past…anything that might name her the daughter of a felon. But she'd over-corrected.

The thing was, her simple mistake on her project had her blame her distraction—the people she'd focused on this week—instead of just taking the mistake as part of life and moving forward. Her little act of walking away from the garage workspace was a reflection of how she'd handled life in general. Not always about her mistakes, though, but the mistakes of those who had hurt her. This whole town seemed to squeeze Molly Jansen out of the state. But really, it was Molly's running that took her away.

They pulled up to Jack's and walked through the garage door to the house. His kitchen was small but opened to the living room. A few toys were scattered on the floor and a baby gate extended across the steps down to the front door.

A tall slender woman with light brown hair, just like Jack's, appeared from a hallway. She put her finger to her lips, then pulled a pocket door and shut off the hallway. Her shoulders slumped, and she said in a hushed voice, "Okay. Now you may speak. Elise is asleep, so still keep it down."

"Thanks for your permission to speak in my own house," Jack sniggered. "Lisa, Molly. Molly, Lisa."

"I remember Lisa," Molly said, thinking his sister was just a taller version of her freshman self.

Lisa's face brightened, and she crossed over and shook hands with Molly. "I remember you too." Molly's own smile wavered, but Lisa just leaned in and said, "My brother was head over heels back then—"

"Lisa, stop meddling." Jack rubbed his cheek and tossed an apologetic look at Molly. Molly's neck grew hot, and she tried to shake it way with a simple flick of her hair. But his sister only confirmed that she had focused so much on mistakes of the past. She'd forgotten the really good parts.

Like Jack.

A door opened at the far end of the living room, and Tate emerged. He noticed Molly right away and ran up to her. "Miss Molly! You're here." His face immediately fell. "But Elise is asleep in my room. You can't help me finish my Lego set."

"That's okay, bud." She tousled his hair. "I don't have a lot of time since my actual building needs some work, but your daddy said I could come say hi."

Jack gave Tate a thumbs-up and then began to talk to Lisa about the new medication.

"Yuck, more medicine." Tate rolled his eyes. He took Molly's hand. "Let me show you around." They headed straight to a bookcase in the half wall that bordered the downstairs foyer.

He picked up a framed picture of Mr. Behrens outside the Corn Crib. "Look, this is my grandpa."

"I know. He used to make the best tenderloin at the Corn Crib."

"You ate there? I wish I could eat there. But Grandpa says he doesn't miss it one bit." Tate frowned. Molly considered what Jack had said about his dad's struggle and noticed Mr. Behrens's unsmiling eyes. Tate dragged her over to the other end of the bookcase. "Look, this is my mom."

A pretty woman sat in a rocking chair, kissing the top of Tate's head. "You were much smaller then," Molly said.

"Yeah, I was only two." They stared at the picture a little longer while Jack and Lisa conversed in the kitchen.

Tate's raspy breathing and the sight of a mom who was robbed of her son's growing up—her son robbed of a mom in his growing up—collided into Molly's heart. Love exuded from Tate's little face as he stared at the picture, just like his mom's beamed with it.

The back door closed. Jack was gone.

Lisa joined Tate and Molly and said, "Jack's just going to check my van. Then you all can be on your way." Molly straightened and raked her hand through her hair. Tate set the picture down and ran across to the door to join his father.

"Brittany showed me how to be a mom." Lisa was eyeing the photo. "And reminded me how important it was to have a rocking chair when Elise came along." She smiled.

"She seems like she was a great lady. It must be really hard for Tate. And Jack."

"Sure is. Has been. But Tate is super resilient. And Jack has been doing really well." Her eyes sparkled. She glanced back at the picture. "Considering. I mean, there would be no grief without love involved, right? All the hurt goes to show how much love resides here."

Molly nodded, but her mind searched for truth in what Lisa had said. If it was true, then she loved her mom more than her resentment would admit. And as far as love was concerned—first suggested by Gran and now mentioned by Jack's younger sister—Molly suspected the love in the Behrens home had just increased by a whole heartful—because love was exactly what she felt for Tate—and love was what she had always felt for Jack.

Molly climbed into Jack's truck, trying to ignore the battle of reality and her feelings. Even if she admitted to the whole world that she was in love with Jack, she'd have to contend with the fact that they couldn't make this work long-term. He'd never get a job near the city, and she'd worked too hard to abandon her position at a prestigious firm. Even the thought of not having the next project on her computer to dream up cast a melancholic cloud over her heart.

Jack started the engine. "I was wondering if we could bring some dinner to you and Gertie tonight? Tate has a big day tomorrow with his appointment, and you will be heading out Friday." He thrust his elbow on the back of the seat between them, turned to see out the back window as he backed out of the garage. She caught his expectant gaze, then cast her eyes down and pulled out her phone from her pocket, trying to tame the wild storm within her.

"Sure. That would be great—" The screen of her phone lit up. She forgot she had turned the sound off. There was a series of texts from Lauren and a missed call from the real estate agent. As she tapped on the voicemail, her battery died. Another frustration added to this day.

"Hey, can I use your charger? I have a voicemail from the real estate agent."

"Sure thing." Jack unplugged his phone and handed it to her while she plugged in hers. "Feel free to check your voicemail on mine."

She smiled, typed in her number to access her voicemail and held the phone to her ear. It smelled like Jack—cedar and mint. She gave him a sideways glance, and he smiled at her. Her whole body relaxed against the seat. Maybe she would be stuck here forever, the decision made. If she could only convince her stubborn work ethic to leave her be.The real estate agent's voice distracted her. "Hi, Molly. This is Sam from JD Realty. I received a generous offer for your grandmother's place—from a corporate farm. Uh, you may have heard of them, Bartle and Sons. They don't even care about the house's condition since it will be converted to offices. The only thing is they would need your farm manager to apply for a position like any other potential employee. No guarantees. Not sure if this interests you, but call me back so I know whether to move forward with getting it on the market."

"Whoa." She ended the call and set his phone on the console.

"What's up?"

"Have you heard of Bartle and Sons?"

"Sure. Who hasn't?" He chuckled. "Well, what farmer hasn't?"

"They made an offer for Gran's place." She studied Jack to see how he might be affected by this news. His whole face went slack and then tightened into a scowl.

Not good. A sour wave sloshed around her stomach.

"They are just a business, Mol. All that work you are doing on Gertie's house to make it an updated home will have gone to waste. Do you really think you want to sell your family farm to a corporation?"

She shrugged. "I guess if the price gives Gran security…and if she doesn't mind."

Jack scoffed. "I am sure she'd care if her home was confiscated for a giant gobbling up farmland across the state."

"Do they farm it?"

"Well, yeah…but it's nothing like a family farm. It's a business."

"Maybe you could find a really good position with a business like that. I am sure their benefits are—"

"No way." Jack sniffed. "I would rather work in an office than have a corporation outline exactly how to do a job I already know how to do. Under someone's thumb while I farm? No, thanks."

"I see. Don't worry, it's just our first offer. I am sure it will all work out." Molly slumped against the seat feeling deflated by Jack's response and hoping this wouldn't be their only option. Especially if Gran would be upset with the end of her house as a home.

Her phone turned on and she scrolled through the texts from Lauren, seeing the last one first:

Molly! You need to call me so I know you got these.

That sour wave in her stomach swelled. What had she missed?

I am really worried, Molly.

What was she talking about? Molly scrolled to the beginning of her texts. Her heart began to race as she read the first text sent right before she had turned the sound off.

Hey, checking in. Looks like everything is moving at record time. You need to be at the property tomorrow at 9 am.

K, I just booked a hotel in Moline tonight. I think you are a good 3 hours from the place. Does that sound ok?

Molly?

Molly's hand flung to her mouth. The cab of the truck closed in on her. This could not be happening.

"I am sorry to be such a downer." Jack's voice was drowned out by the loud pumping in Molly's ears.

"No worries…" Her own voice sounded like it was a mile down the road. She continued to scroll.

Hey, this is pretty important. Sounds like the client doesn't just want a PowerPoint but hard copies since you'll be in a rural area. Will you be able to get your design printed out?

Looks like a print shop opens at 6 am in Moline.

"Oh no. This can't be happening." Molly clutched at the door as Jack pulled down Gran's driveway.

"What can't be happening?" Jack shifted into Park just in front of the garage.

Molly yanked the door handle and jumped down onto the gravel. "Work stuff. I have to get my computer."

"Molly, you are pale. Did something bad happen?" Jack hopped out of his side of the truck and started around toward her.

She dodged him coming closer. He'd distracted her enough. This was way more important than some revived love story. She hadn't seen the need for a reality check until this very minute, when her messed-up project sat on her computer and her chance of a lifetime grew more and more distant. "I have so much to do. I-I just can't—"

She rushed past him and ran across the flagstone path to the garage door.

"See you tonight!" Jack called out.

As she opened the door to go inside, Molly watched him walk back around his truck and slide behind the wheel. He waved, and she waved back.

Molly stood at the door longer than she should, unable to process everything that had happened and was about to happen.

But she couldn't waste time.

Two thoughts crossed her mind as she entered the dim garage and gathered up her computer and notepad. First, if that offer was a good one, it might just be worth considering. No more remodeling, and Gran would get to her sister sooner than later. And second, there was no way she would be seeing Jack tonight.

Molly was more certain than ever that she would need to just talk herself out of whatever love she felt for a man who would always be hundreds of miles away.

Chapter Twenty

Jack drove to the steel building to finish up before heading home to grab Tate. He didn't like the panic in Molly's voice, and he was worried about the offer for Austin Farm. He wasn't that concerned about a corporation snatching up the property, but Bartle and Sons was known for questionable ethics. When they went to Gertie's for dinner tonight, he would explain to Molly.

Over the next couple of hours, Jack caught himself praying for Molly—and not for her change of heart to make this relationship work. He prayed that whatever she was struggling with would work itself out. By the time he headed back home to get Tate and pick up some food at the BBQ Shack, Jack was more anxious than ever to get to Gertie's and make sure Molly was okay.

When Tate and Jack pulled in the driveway, the afternoon sun lit up the front of the house, cutting a sharp contrast between the shadowy corner with the swing and the rest of the porch. Gertie sat on the swing. Jack couldn't quite figure out what was amiss as he parked.

Tate jumped out of the truck and ran to the porch.

Gertie didn't stand, just held out her hands for Tate to give her a hug.

Jack took the two sacks of food from the back seat. A waft of savory aroma coaxed his stomach to growl. He crossed over to the newly painted porch. "Hey there, Gertie." He took the steps two at a time and set the bags by the door. Tate climbed up on the swing.

The look on Gertie's face stole away any appetite. "Thanks for the food." Her smile didn't reach her eyes, and her nostrils were red. He noticed a balled-up tissue in her hand. "We'll have plenty of leftovers."

Jack inhaled sharply and turned on his heel realizing what was missing. Molly's car. "Where's Molly?"

"She asked me to tell you goodbye." She turned to Tate and put her hand on his knee. "Miss Molly was really sorry not to see you tonight. But said she'll be thinking superhero thoughts for you tomorrow." Her glassy gaze landed on Jack. "And she said she'll miss you very much."

Jack shook his head. "Wait, she can't just leave. There's still stuff to fix up before the walk-through on Saturday."

Gertie sighed. "We talked about that. It seems like we don't have to fix up anything after all—"

"What?" Jack snapped. "Don't tell me you are going with Bartle and Sons?"

Gertie gave a curt nod.

Jack swiped his hat off and ran a hand through his hair. He was about to mention Rob's own disdain for that company but caught his outburst with a groan. Mentioning that to his widow would be heartless and unnecessary.

"Why did she leave?" He spoke through his teeth.

There was something more than the offer causing Molly alarm. "She seemed shaken when I dropped her off today."

Gertie fiddled with the tissue. "There's a big meeting for her tomorrow. She was hysterical that she'd run out of time to present her best. After I calmed her down, we talked about our options. It didn't seem right to drag this out any longer." She stood. "Jack, every day is just one more day of reminders. It seemed like perfect timing for Molly to carry on with her work and for me to get out of this place." She cast a glance around the porch, landing on the post that Jack and Molly had worked on together. "I also want you to know that I will write a letter of outstanding recommendation for you to send to Bartle and Sons. You can still work this land—"

"Absolutely not." He had promised himself to take care of Gertie like Rob would want him to, and he thought he'd done a decent job. He might not tell Gertie how disappointed her husband would be with this development, but he would certainly not entertain being part of this future for Austin Farm. Or, more likely, its devastating end.

Gertie drew close to Jack, casting a quick glance down at Tate, then blocking Jack's view of his son. She spoke in a hushed voice. "Molly said she'd pay for movers to pack everything and unpack at the retirement community. I asked her about coming by one last time to see you all." She laid a hand on Jack's shoulder. "Jack, I saw the pain in her eyes. I do believe she cares for you more than she might admit. If you feel the same about her, then I suggest not putting another decade between you two. Life is much too short." She patted him, then opened the door.

Jack picked up the sacks and followed her through to the kitchen with Tate moping alongside him.

"I miss Miss Molly," he huffed.

"Come on, superhero. Let's get the table all set." Gertie swooped in and guided Tate by the shoulders with a sniffle or two.

Jack may have been foolish to consider trading his dream of farming for a chance to be with Molly, but now he was cornered by a future of office life with not one perk but a paycheck.

If she had just stuck around for one last dinner, he could have at least convinced her to wait for a solid farmer to buy the place.

As he set the sacks on the counter and began to unload containers of baked beans, mashed potatoes and pulled pork, he remembered that Molly had used his phone to check her voice mail.

She was just a text away.

He pulled his phone out, scrolled through his recent calls, added her to his contacts, then opened a new text message.

His fingers paused above the screen. What would he say? Tell her to get back here and find a decent buyer for the farm? Wouldn't she think Jack was trying to avoid the inevitable—a goodbye and unemployment?

Molly was doing what she had set out to do all along. Returning to Chicago to live out her dream. Jack wondered if he'd be happy with anyone buying up the property if it meant Molly's last visit to Polk Center was close at hand.

If he texted her now, he'd only confirm why she hadn't wanted to commit to a long-distance relationship. Being torn between two places wasn't the way to live. She was the practical one. And he was the fool.

Besides, he'd been praying for her all afternoon. Jack had already come to the conclusion that only God could work this out, anyway. His revived faith was pretty slippery.

He deleted the message draft and laid a heavy palm on the counter. He couldn't push things along nor convince God that his plan was better. It seemed that Molly was on her way to the biggest promotion of her life, and Jack was heading for a career change.

As they loaded up their plates and circled around Gertie's kitchen table, Jack tried to be grateful that he'd received an interview with the seed company after all. But all Jack felt was sorrow. The same sorrow he'd seen on Molly's face the day he broke up with her. The only difference was this time Molly was off to bigger and better things, and Jack was the brokenhearted one, still trying to piece his life together amid old grief and new.

Molly sat at a hotel desk with a coffee, a half-eaten panini and a whole bunch of changes to make on her screen. She'd spent the whole drive brainstorming how she could adjust the design but keep intact the precision and simplicity of the structure. However, her thoughts were sabotaged with all that had happened these past couple of weeks. Work and home were intertwining in her mind like a sneaky vine choking out her peace. Polk Center in her rearview mirror wasn't nearly as satisfying as it used to be.

Molly couldn't help but think she was running away again. As she drove, she tried to convince herself to not be triggered by the condemning thought like she had on

Jack's porch. But the lie crept into her conscience and blared the accusation that she was her mother's daughter—a label she could never run away from. Last time she was on this road, the fact wasn't so clear—she'd spent the last decade trying to do exactly that.

But seeing the picture of Jack's dad in Tate's tiny hands reminded her what Jack had said about his father's hidden struggle during Brittany's illness. Jack didn't know what his dad was going through until he'd let resentment build.

Molly was only eight when Mom first left, and a teenager when her mom's final escapade thrust her out of Polk Center for good. She'd never had the chance to ask Mom exactly what she struggled with. And she might never get to on this side of Heaven.

But something shifted in Molly's heart when she considered that Mom's mistakes might be rooted in something much deeper than a disregard for her daughter. Like Molly's project would be proof of chipping away the rough to get to the diamond, maybe Mom hadn't found the tools needed to slough away whatever hard stuff was keeping her down.

When Molly turned into a gas station halfway to Moline, she prayed that God would work in Mom's life and that He'd help Molly find forgiveness too. She didn't feel anything resembling forgiveness as she hopped out of the car, but she felt a sputter of peace as she filled her tank.

The rest of the way, Molly's old habit of sifting through the reasons why she should never return to Polk Center seemed to only turn up reasons why she should go back. And if her heart wouldn't jump-start and race like a giddy schoolgirl at reason number one—Jack Behrens—she'd be able to redirect her thoughts to the appropriate focus—straight ahead. More than once, though, she fantasized about pulling through a rest stop and taking a left instead of a right.

That was dangerous thinking. And her resurrected teenage pastime of dreaming was one reason she should keep Polk Center in the rearview mirror for good. Passing up this chance to prove her worth in Chicago would cause her to lose so much.

She looked around the hotel room. Modern, straight-edged, perfectly polished. Molly took a swig of her lukewarm oat milk honey latte. Sweet and creamy. The drink was her regular at her own corner coffee shop. She squeezed her eyes tight and tried to drum up a nostalgic wave for her real home in Chicago.

It might take another decade to find love for her loft and lifestyle like she'd found beneath an Iowa sky. That was okay. She had nothing to lose by waiting.

She released a breath and drew her face closer to the screen.

As she worked on the last change before sending the whole thing to the printers, impatience proved her plan to wait was a little too idealistic. If she was honest with herself, love was the main difference between Chicago and Polk Center.

In that case, Chicago–0, Polk Center–3.

She couldn't help but laugh. Jack was the athlete, not her. Her pulse sped up, and she pushed back in her chair. What would he do if he knew she kept score in his favor like that? A silly smile crept on Molly's face. He'd wrap his arms around her and beg her to stay.

Once long ago, she'd dreamed that up in her mind, when the football player said goodbye. Every step outside of Polk Center, she'd hoped he'd follow her and ask her to make the long-distance work.

That was probably her last teenage fantasy.

College life began to refine her for less frivolous thinking. Look how far she'd come. It was time to prove to herself that all the distance between Molly and Polk Center was a very good thing.

Chapter Twenty-One

Molly's six-o'clock alarm seemed to go off as soon as she fell asleep. She had gone to bed at two in the morning once she finally sent her project to the printers via email. After confirming that the print shop had received it, they guaranteed to have the prints ready in an hour. Molly hopped in the shower, cranked up her music on her phone as she usually did during her morning routine. A smidge back to who she was pre–Austin farmhouse makeover. Yes. This felt right.

She didn't love that her most appropriate work attire was the black dress she'd worn to Grandad's funeral, but once she considered how much he'd bragged on her to his friends, she felt differently. Any memory of Grandad would boost her spirits. He was her inspiration more than she ever knew. She was thankful for that realization which might have been lost had she never returned to Austin Farm.

Molly headed downstairs to the hotel lobby, grabbed a croissant and a coffee to go, then set out to the printers. Once she checked over the prints, rolled them into her case in the trunk and set out for the property, adrenaline set in full force. She practiced her presentation over and over out loud, finishing up the third time round when her GPS said *You've arrived.*

Her boss's BMW was parked by a picnic area, next to two other cars. She suspected the property owner claimed the Tesla and the Toyota pickup was her competition's. Pulling up on the other side of the Tesla, anxiety unleashed within her. Had they already rubbed elbows enough to discount her altogether? She rushed out of the car and slung her print case over her shoulder.

Voices mingled with the ripples of the river. Just up from where she parked, the three men stood facing west. The owner was speaking with his arms. When her boss, Mr. Lockner, glanced her way, he gently directed the attention to her with a nod.

"Here is Miss Jansen now." He took long strides toward her. "I am very excited to see what you've come up with." He beamed. Molly couldn't help but mirror his smile. She was thrilled that he was excited, and she couldn't ignore that her competitor, Harleson, observed with a tight-lipped smile.

"Ah, is this the grand experiment?" The property owner wore skinny jeans and an untucked collared shirt. His mirrored sunglasses reflected a tiny Mr. Lockner and an even tinier Molly.

Molly's stomach did a nervous flip. "Experiment?"

"I was sharing with Phil that you are our first employee to work remotely for the firm. Your situation gave us the perfect opportunity to test this."

"I hope I don't let you down."

"Well, being able to make this meeting is a very good sign. Part of our hesitation in allowing for working from home was lack of flexibility on these types of impromptu decisions."

"I would never miss this chance," Molly assured him. The owner turned the conversation to the property again. Molly soaked up the setting. She tried to imagine her building perched on this gem of land, with a swath of trees buffering the riverbank and the roll of the land exactly how she had pictured it.

A picnic table was set with an outdoor tablecloth and an ice chest of bottled water and boxed deli lunches. Harleson gave his presentation of a more rugged design, using some of the historical aspects of the area, as well as the nearby architectural elements of existing homes in his exterior elements. Molly presented her work the same way she had practiced in the car. She was thankful for Jack when the use of the diamond-in-the-rough analogy gained a little more enthusiasm from Mr. Lockner and the owner than at the beginning of her presentation.

After eating and discussing that final decisions would be made at the office, they walked to their cars. Mr. Lockner approached Molly while she put her case back in the trunk.

"You know, I expected a different direction from you, Molly." He crossed his arms over his plaid button-up and hooked his finger on his chin. "This was a little sterile."

All the adrenaline and excitement of the morning collapsed to her ballet-slippered feet.

"Don't get me wrong, the design was beautiful, but there just didn't seem to be any heart in it. As if you were trying too hard to lean into a concept instead of tapping into a sense of home."

"Home?"

"Yes, a place where you can relax and settle in. Your

design was more of a structure. Heart, connection—that's what makes a home."

Molly shook her head as her throat tightened. "I think I just need more time. I was really looking forward to our consultation. I am very willing to change whatever you'd like."

"That's what I like about you, Molly. You will do what it takes. I don't doubt it." He began to walk to his car. "We'll find the right project for you. There's no rush."

Molly slid into the driver's seat and placed shaky hands on the wheel. She had just spent almost two weeks in a place that was filled to the brim with heart and connection. How had she missed incorporating such key features of home into her project? All this time, she had focused on accomplishing the next goal. She had stashed away her savings and inheritance for the next goal—a high-end condo—but even that wouldn't bring her closer to the nostalgic feeling that only Austin Farm evoked.

It seemed that Molly Jansen had sloughed off so much of her hurt and past that she was left with a heartless diamond, one that would only keep her striving in a no-rush position, when all she wanted was to race ahead. Would she ever be satisfied with the next accomplishment? She hadn't been looking for kudos, she'd been looking for peace. And there was only one place she'd found it lately. Gran and Jack appeared in her thoughts. They had constantly appreciated her beyond any accomplishment. And the love she had found brought her a glimpse of peace she'd been craving all these years. And then there was Tate. The little guy had filled Gran's house with so much life that his absence was sorely missed.

Molly gasped. She flung her door open and ran over to Mr. Lockner's car. He was just about to pull out. She waved her hands through his rearview window and his brake lights lit up.

He rolled his window down.

"I am sorry, sir. I didn't mean to startle you. But I know you are right. I just spent two weeks in a place that was filled to the brim with heart." He lifted his sunglasses onto his head and gave her a quizzical look. "I am just wondering, what would it take for me to continue working out of an old Iowa farmhouse?"

"For how long?"

Molly shrugged her shoulders. "Well, there's no rush, right? And I promise to continue to do whatever it takes. That's just who I am."

After the rough news from last night, Jack focused on Tate's appointment. Even though Tate was under the weather, his testing went well, and his lung function was decent. Jack and Tate arrived at Gertie's to celebrate the good news with cupcakes—a quarterly-appointment tradition.

When Gertie welcomed them inside, she was splattered in paint.

"Answered prayers," she exclaimed after Tate excitedly told her his numbers. She held his cheeks with both hands and kissed his forehead. "I am so glad." Tate climbed up in the kitchen chair with his drawing pad, crayons and a cupcake already licked clear of frosting.

"The doctor was really encouraging," Jack said as he leaned against the counter while Gertie poured glasses of iced tea. "Said to keep up the good work."

"You've done so well with him." Gertie handed him some tea.

"I couldn't do it without you and Lisa." He sipped the

slightly sweet, cool drink. "Got an interview tomorrow at the seed company to stay in Polk Center."

"Well, that's nice." Her brow furrowed, but she managed a smile.

"Seems like you might not agree with that?" He chuckled but wondered if he agreed with that too.

"I just thought you'd try and keep farming."

"The opportunities for that are too far away from you all. From Lisa and all her help."

"Sure, she's a great help. But Jack, you are a great father. And farmer. I am sure you will look out for Tate, no matter who is around to help."

He cocked his head in her direction. "Are you trying to kick me out of Polk Center?"

She laughed and patted his arm. "I just want you to follow your heart."

Jack's face drained, and he swallowed hard.

"Farming. That's your heart, isn't it?" Gertie sipped her tea. Wide sea-green eyes peered over her glass. Was she sincere…or hinting?

"Yes, but I was willing to put that on hold for security right now. An office job will give me that."

Gertie set her glass down and began to clean up Tate's cupcake wrapper. "In that case, there are plenty of office jobs between here and… Chicago?" She didn't look at him as she crossed over to the waste bin, but her smile was not discreet.

"Gertie Austin, what are you getting at?" He set his glass down and crossed his arms over a pounding heartbeat.

She squared her shoulders and stood directly in front of him. Her amusement was replaced by determination. "The way I see it, you have told yourself this story that you aren't an adequate caregiver for your son. I've seen you, Jack. You are the most attentive daddy I've ever known. Yes. Ever. If Polk Center doesn't offer you a career…or your heart's desire—" Her mouth corners twitched, and her lashes wobbled. "The only person stopping you is you." She poked his bicep.

"If you think I should intrude on your granddaughter's life in Chicago by getting an office job—"

"Intrude?" Gertie laughed and tossed her head back. "Didn't I tell you how upset Molly was when she decided to leave? You think it was because of this old house?" She shook her head. "She loves you, Jack Behrens. Take it from an old woman who spent fifty years with the love of her life. I can tell love when I see it." Her eyes swam as her words landed like drops of rain on his heart's thirsty soil.

He pushed his chin up and had to admit, "I love her too, Gertie. More than I ever thought I could love again." He shrugged his shoulders in surrender. Surrender to all the doubt and deception of only needing to survive. He'd endured so much hard stuff already; wasn't it about time he enjoyed life again? While God had done a mighty work on Austin Farm, Jack realized he had some responsibility in helping the harvest along.

Jack knew exactly what he needed to do.

He wiped his eyes with his knuckles, then inhaled a jagged breath. Without looking away from Gertie's beaming face, he said, "Tate, want to stay with Gran today? I think I have a long drive ahead of me."

Chapter Twenty-Two

The anticipation when she first pulled up to the client's property paled compared to the energy buzzing through Molly now. Mr. Lockner had agreed to try out telecommuting for a trial run, and Molly took that as a different kind of promotion. She might not be inching her way up the corporate ladder, but there was something more important she was heading toward.

As she turned onto the highway, Molly debated whether to call Gran and share with her that they wouldn't be selling to Bartle and Sons. Especially after she'd hung up with the real estate agent. They'd worked out the details of what it would take to keep the farm running and what monthly payments might be for the mortgage. Her nest egg would be a sufficient down payment without a penny to spare, but Molly didn't care.

She was going home at last.

Molly never dreamed that she would be excited to see that *The People of Iowa Welcome You* sign. Last time she passed it, she'd imagined the sneers and name-calling by her high-school peers.

Those people were her people. And Molly Jansen was

beyond proud to claim them as her own. Well, maybe not Chelle or the other folks who hadn't taken the time to get to know her back then, but she could think of one who she prayed and hoped would be willing to take her back. Remorse overwhelmed her as she considered standing Jack up last night for dinner. Sure, they were going to eat with Tate and Gran, but she didn't give him the chance to say goodbye. She didn't give Tate the chance to say goodbye.

Molly gripped the steering wheel tight and prayed that God would work in their hearts to forgive her. She knew what it was like to lose someone without the consideration of a goodbye. If Jack would take her back, she'd spend the rest of her life trying to make up for any heartache she caused. And just like Molly could be depended on to do what it took to get work accomplished and life to the next level, she would be the same with Jack. He was her heart. Life with him was the one fantasy she had stashed away not realizing it could grow into this dream-come-true.

The sign on the Iowa border appeared, and Molly resisted pressing the gas beyond what the speed limit would allow. The drive across the bridge was as slow as the pace of the Mississippi below. Molly groaned and wondered exactly how she would spend the next three hours without a speeding ticket or giving in and asking Gran for Jack's number.

At that thought, her phone rang.

It was a central Iowa area code. Maybe it was the real estate agent. The number was not familiar, though.

"This is Molly."

"Hey, where are you heading so fast?" Jack's voice

jump-started her heart at a speed well past warranting a ticket. "I thought you were in Chicago."

"Uh, how do you know I'm heading—"

"I am standing here watching you disappear over the horizon."

"What?" Molly glanced in the rearview mirror and looked over her shoulder. "What are you talking about?"

"See that rest stop back there on the right?"

Molly glimpsed a building slip just past the horizon. "Are you seriously there?"

"Waiting for you, Mol. I've spent a long time waiting for you without even knowing it." His voice was rich, warm, the very essence of home.

"Seems like you and I have been doing the same thing." Molly pressed on her brakes when she saw a left turn ahead. "It's about time we stop waiting, don't you think?"

"I'll be here…waiting still."

The call ended, and Molly drove back and pulled into the rest stop. Jack was leaning on his truck, the early-afternoon sun accentuating his tan. Same cutoff ISU shirt from almost two weeks ago, same muscles. Totally different tidal wave of emotion.

She jerked her car into Park and hopped out. Jack stood at her door, his John Deere hat pulled over piercing eyes. "I-I was coming to you, Molly."

"What do you mean?"

"If I am going to get a cubicle job, Illinois has just as many as Iowa."

"You were going to move to Chicago?"

He shrugged and those dimples appeared with a dazzling smile. "Sure?" He chuckled. "Molly, I want to give us a chance. No matter where. I think I have Tate's blessing." He pulled out a piece of paper. Molly took it. A drawing of a superhero little boy sandwiched between a stick figure with a baseball cap and a shorter stick figure with a laptop.

A laugh burst from her lips. "What a sweetheart."

Jack offered his hand to her. She took it. "Hey, we were sweethearts once. Can we try it again?"

Molly melted against his chest, slid her palm on his shaved jaw and pulled him close, boomeranging her gaze from his loving eyes to his waiting lips. Softly she said, "We've got all the time in the world now."

He kissed her gently on the mouth, then the nose, then held up her hand and kissed her knuckles. "I love you, Molly Jansen. In Chicago, in Polk Center...doesn't matter. I just love you."

Molly tilted her head, ready to make this farmer's dream come true. "You don't need to move, Jack."

"I want to. I want to be with you. Whatever it takes."

She giggled and pulled away. "I am keeping Austin Farm. The real estate agent's getting the paperwork ready."

Jack cupped his hand on his mouth, paced away, then turned to her with misty eyes. "What about your job?"

"Well, that's the thing. An amazing handyman set up the internet at my farmhouse."

He shook his head and raised an eyebrow. "*Your* farmhouse?"

Molly took Jack's arms and placed them around her waist again. "The perfect office for me. But I'll need to hire a farm manager. Do you know of one?"

Jack's arms tightened as he buried his face in her neck and twirled her around. "I can't believe this." The joy in his voice filled Molly's heart to the brim.

He set her on her feet, and she cupped her hands around his neck. "I love you, Jack. I think I always have, and I know that I always will." He kissed her again.

With a long drive ahead, following the farmer of her dreams, Molly Jansen thanked God that her architecture dream and her Iowa roots were finally growing together to make a perfect match.

* * * * *

Dear Reader,

There is so much I'd like to share with you about my inspiration for Molly and Jack's story. First, my family and I have lived in central Iowa for over a decade, and Iowa has become very special to us. We enjoy summers admiring sunbathed cornfields, sampling sweet Dutch pastries and spending cool nights at the ball field. Also, having a background in architecture and a husband who works in agriculture, I just couldn't resist giving my first contemporary-romance couple similar interests. Yes, I married a farm boy, and actually, his late grandparents lived in a historic farmhouse in Texas. I cherish my memories in that home and often marvel at the Iowa farmhouses sporting the same white paint and covered porches.

Finally, my inspiration for Tate comes from a longtime friendship with the family of a cystic fibrosis superhero. My family and I have had several opportunities to support him and others through various Cystic Fibrosis Foundation events. Please check out this amazing organization's website, www.cff.org.

Thank you for reading this special story. If you would like updates on my future books, please sign up for my newsletter at www.angiedicken.com.

Sincerely,
Angie Dicken

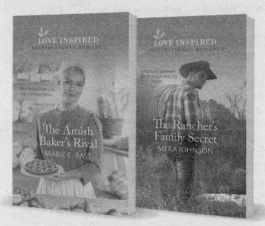

COMING NEXT MONTH FROM
Love Inspired

AN AMISH PROPOSAL FOR CHRISTMAS
Indiana Amish Market • by Vannetta Chapman

Assistant store manager Rebecca Yoder is determined to see the world and put Shipshewana, Indiana, behind her. The only thing standing in her way is training new hire Gideon Fisher and convincing him the job's a dream. But will he delay her exit or convince her to stay?

HER SURPRISE CHRISTMAS COURTSHIP
Seven Amish Sisters • by Emma Miller

Millie Koffman dreams of becoming a wife and mother someday. But because of her plus size, she doubts it will ever come true—especially not with handsome neighbor Elden Yoder. But when Elden shows interest in her, Millie's convinced it's a ruse. Can she learn to love herself before she loses the man loves?

THE VETERAN'S HOLIDAY HOME
K-9 Companions • by Lee Tobin McClain

After a battlefield incident leaves him injured and unable to serve, veteran Jason Smith resolves to spend his life guiding troubled boys with the help of his mastiff, Titan. Finding the perfect opportunity at the school Bright Tomorrows means working with his late brother's widow, principal Ashley Green...*if* they can let go of the past.

JOURNEY TO FORGIVENESS
Shepherd's Creek • by Danica Favorite

Inheriting failing horse stables from her estranged father forces Josie Shepherd to return home and face her past—including her ex-love. More than anything, Brady King fervently regrets ever hurting Josie. Could saving the stables together finally bring peace to them—and maybe something more?

THE BABY'S CHRISTMAS BLESSING
by Meghann Whistler

Back on Cape Cod after an eleven-year absence, Steve Weston is desperate for a nanny to help care for his newborn nephew. When the lone candidate turns out to be Chloe Richardson, the woman whose heart he shattered when they were teens, he'll have to choose between following his heart or keeping his secrets...

SECOND CHANCE CHRISTMAS
by Betsy St. Amant

Blake Bryant left small-town life behind him with no intention of going back—until he discovers the niece he never knew about is living in a group foster home. But returning to Tulip Mound also involves seeing Charlie Bussey, the woman who rejected him years ago. Can he open his heart enough to let them both in?

————————

LOOK FOR THESE AND OTHER LOVE INSPIRED BOOKS WHEREVER BOOKS ARE SOLD, INCLUDING MOST BOOKSTORES, SUPERMARKETS, DISCOUNT STORES AND DRUGSTORES.

LICNM0822

HARLEQUIN
PLUS

Announcing a **BRAND-NEW**
multimedia subscription service
for romance fans like you!

Read, Watch and Play.

Experience the easiest way to get
the romance content you crave.

Start your **FREE 7 DAY TRIAL** at
<u>www.harlequinplus.com/freetrial</u>.

SPECIAL EXCERPT FROM

LOVE INSPIRED
INSPIRATIONAL ROMANCE

When a wounded veteran and his service dog seek work at the Bright Tomorrows school for troubled boys, can the principal—who happens to be the widow of his late brother—hire the man who knows the past secrets she'd rather forget?

Read on for a sneak peek at
The Veteran's Holiday Home
by Lee Tobin McClain!

Jason stared at the woman in the doorway of the principal's office. "*You're* A. Green?"

Just looking at her sent shock waves through him. What had happened to his late brother's wife?

She was still gorgeous, no doubt. But she was much thinner than she'd been when he'd last seen her, her strong cheekbones standing out above full lips, still pretty although now without benefit of lipstick. She wore a business suit, the blouse underneath buttoned up to her chin.

Her eyes still had that vulnerable look in them, though, the one that had sucked him into making a mistake, doing what he shouldn't have done. Making a phone call with disastrous results.

She recovered before he did. "Come in. You'll want to sit down," she said. "I'm sorry about Ricky running into you and your dog."

He followed her into her office.

He waited for her to sit behind her desk before easing himself into a chair. He wasn't supposed to lift anything above fifty pounds and he wasn't supposed to twist, and the way his back felt right now, after doing both, proved his orthopedic doctor was right.

Beside him, Titan whined and moved closer, and Jason put a hand on the big dog. "Lie down," he ordered, but gently. Titan had saved him from a bad fall.

LIEXP0822

"I didn't realize the two of you knew each other," the secretary said. "Can I get you both some coffee?"

"We're fine," Ashley said, and even though Jason had been about to decline the offer, he looked a question at her. Was she too hostile to even give a man a beverage?

The older woman backed out of the office. The door clicked shut.

Leaving Ashley and Jason alone.

"The website didn't have a picture—" he began.

"You always went by Jason in the family—" she said at the same time.

They both laughed awkwardly.

"You really didn't know it was me who'd be interviewing you?" she asked, her voice skeptical.

"No. Your website's kind of…limited."

If he'd known the job would involve working with his late half brother's wife, he'd never have applied. Too many bad memories, and while he'd been fortunate to come out of the combat zone with fewer mental health issues than some vets, he had to watch his frame of mind, take care about the kind of environment he lived in. That was one reason he'd liked the looks of this job, high in the Colorado Rocky Mountains. He needed to get out of the risky neighborhood where he was living.

Ashley presented a different kind of risk.

Being constantly reminded of his brilliant, successful younger brother, so much more suave and popular and talented than Jason was, at least on the outside…being reminded of the difficulties of his home life after his mom had married Christopher's dad…no. He'd escaped all that, and no way was he going back.

His own feelings for his brother's wife notwithstanding. He'd felt sorry for her, had tried to help, but she'd spurned his help and pushed him away.

Getting involved with her was a mistake he wouldn't make again.

Don't miss
The Veteran's Holiday Home *by Lee Tobin McClain,*
available October 2022
wherever Love Inspired books and ebooks are sold.

LoveInspired.com

LIEXP0822